SLEEPING TIGER

BY

LINDA DENNIS

Copyright © LINDA DENNIS 2019
This book is sold subject to the condition that it shall not, by way of trade or otherwise, be lent, resold, hired out, or otherwise circulated without the publisher's prior consent in any form of binding or cover other than that in which it is published and without a similar condition including this condition being imposed on the subsequent publisher.
The moral right of LINDA DENNIS has been asserted.
ISBN-13: 9781095199701

This is a work of fiction. Names, characters, businesses, organisations, places, events and incidents either are the product of the author's imagination or are used fictitiously. Any resemblance to actual persons, living or dead, events, or locales is entirely coincidental.

DEDICATION

*Dedicated to all the young people/adults
who inspired me to write.*

CONTENTS

Chapter 1 .... *1*
Chapter 2 .... *11*
Chapter 3 .... *21*
Chapter 4 .... *31*
Chapter 5 .... *39*
Chapter 6 .... *49*
Chapter 7 .... *59*
Chapter 8 .... *69*
Chapter 9 .... *79*
Chapter 10 .... *90*
Chapter 11 .... *98*
Chapter 12 .... *108*
Chapter 13 .... *120*
Chapter 14 .... *130*
Chapter 15 .... *140*
Chapter 16 .... *149*
Chapter 17 .... *159*
Chapter 18 .... *169*
Chapter 19 .... *180*
Chapter 20 .... *190*
Chapter 21 .... *200*
Chapter 22 .... *209*
Chapter 23 .... *219*
Chapter 24 .... *229*
Chapter 25 .... *239*
Chapter 26 .... *249*
Chapter 27 .... *259*
Epilogue *267*
ABOUT THE AUTHOR *270*

ACKNOWLEDGMENTS

All thanks to my husband for consistently reading and checking my work!

Chapter 1

With an almighty tug, Kirstin pulled out the suitcase from the top of the wardrobe. Unfortunately, several other items came with it. Sighing, she plonked the suitcase down and knelt to pick up a box and its lid. The contents of the box were sprawled all over the pale pink carpet and she knew immediately what they were. Loose photographs lay spread like fans with images she would rather not have cast her eyes over.

The smiling faces of her friends and family stared back at her, as did that of her ex-husband. The photos were a mixture of her wedding, school days, family holidays and her much-loved pets, who had sadly passed on. All of which triggered sadness, joy, anger and a feeling of melancholy.

She gingerly picked up the photos but frequently

stopped and stared at some in detail. It took her mind back over several years of happy and unhappy memories. She wasn't the most confident person. She had little self-esteem in those days and was easily swayed and influenced by those who were in authority or in control.

The last photo was placed in the box. It was a photo of three children. Kirstin was in the middle of a boy and another girl. It showed the results of the second Cadbury's Handwriting Competition.

This was where the winner would receive five limited edition deep purple boxes, which when pushed from the bottom slid smoothly upwards, revealing tantalisingly tiny, individually wrapped bars of Cadbury's Dairy Milk Chocolate as their prize.

They looked splendid, all lined up like soldiers in their boxes; neat, tidy and flawless. This was the most desirable prize for any perfectionist, particularly someone as punctilious as Kirstin.

Kirstin Alexander had entered this competition for two consecutive years and on both occasions had come second. Nothing unusual about that really, as coming second best was unfortunately to become a common trait for Kirstin, but when she was 11 years old this seemed like the end of the world. With hindsight, it was incredibly clear to her that these feelings never change, no matter how old you are, they just become proportionate to life at the time; sometimes creating absolutely no feelings whatsoever and at other times popping into the mind on all manner of occasions, causing disgruntlement for days.

The Cadbury's Chocolate Handwriting Competition had taken her back on a long journey of disappointing memories, lack of achievement and denial of love and attention, both as a child and a young adult.

These recurring memories immediately instigated a steady stream of past emotional pathways that her life had taken over the years. Now at 60, Kirstin wanted closure and needed to let go of all such regret and heartache.

Today Kirstin was on a train to London where she was meeting an old friend, Susannah Kingsley. Susannah had never married but had a partner, Greg Morton, with whom she had lived with for 35 years. Susannah had just retired. She had been a journalist on a national newspaper and was very highly thought of within her field. Greg also worked on the same newspaper as an editorial producer but he had decided to stay for a couple more years, until he was 65.

Kirstin had arranged to spend Thursday night at Susannah and Greg's house in Barnes and on Friday, she and Susannah would travel to Monaco for a few days' celebration break away, for her 60th birthday.

Phil, Kirstin's husband of 25 years, had suggested

this treat as he knew how Kirstin had always wanted to visit Monaco. It had never appealed to him, so he was happy to pay for both to have a few days together, to chat, catch up and of course have some retail therapy. It wasn't Kirstin's birthday until she returned home in early March, so they would be having their own celebrations together and with family later. Phil had felt that retiring from her job as Head of Psychology at Leeds University, and shortly to reach sixty were very good reasons to have a timely break with a girlfriend to relax, enjoy and plan future events. *A very considerate gesture*, Kirstin had thought.

Kirstin glanced away from staring out of the train window and could see the ticket collector making his way down the carriage. She rummaged in her brand-new Chanel handbag, which she'd bought herself as an early retirement gift, to find her purse and quickly located her ticket, which she placed on the table in front of her ready. She didn't notice the ticket collector take her ticket nor clip the edge of it and place it back on the table, as she had again drifted into looking out of the window and was immersed back in the past.

She was never a high flyer academically at school but she did enjoy her time there and would have enjoyed it more if she'd had the support, encouragement and interest of her parents. The only salvation was that at the age of 14, she met someone who would eventually mean a great deal to her, but for the moment this began as a platonic relationship and kept her sane and uplifted. For the next few years, life was good as a teenager although without being aware of it, Max Tarrant, her constant companion and confidante, since fourteen, had already started to manipulate Kirstin in a way she was unable to recognise or even consider. He was everything she needed. He gave her guidance, advice, and discussed what direction in life to consider and what to work towards to seek out a chosen destiny. Max held all the answers to anything she wished to know, and this satisfied her and gave her a great feeling of protection. Unfortunately, she was putting him on a pedestal where he certainly wasn't going to be knocked off for some time yet.

The train pulled into King's Cross and as Kirstin disembarked she glanced in the direction of the exit at the end of the platform, not that anyone was meeting her. She had agreed to jump in a taxi to Barnes as it was easier for everyone for her to arrive in this way.

She stared as a tall dark-haired man started to walk in her direction. Kirstin froze and stopped walking. She could feel her heart pounding. *Why has he come to meet me? How would he know I was on this train?* These questions reeled in her head. Max had always met her at King's Cross station when she had come down from Leeds and he had been in his first year at the

London School of Economics. This was over forty years ago, how could this be happening now?

Kirstin could see this man quite clearly now as he approached her and realised immediately that it wasn't Max at all and that he was about to walk straight past her to greet a lady behind her, who had several large cases and was waiting for his assistance. She still couldn't move from the spot where she was standing and was visibly shaken. A passing guard asked if she needed any help. She thanked him but declined.

She walked slowly to the exit and to where she could see a sign directing her to the taxi rank to join a small queue over in the far corner of the station. It had been a long time since she had been in King's Cross station and it was extremely different, almost unrecognisable from all those years ago. She gazed in amazement at 'Searcy's Grand Brassiere and Champagne Bar' and thought how chic, sophisticated and truly lovely to find this at a train station. After the sudden shock, premonition, flashback or whatever it was, that had just occurred, she felt she could do with a glass of champagne or certainly a drink but that was for later she thought and smiled.

That evening Kirstin disclosed the incident at King's Cross station to Susannah, whilst Greg was finishing his shower, having just got in from work. Their taxi would be here in 20 minutes, so ample time to finish their glasses of champagne and for Kirstin to bring Susannah up to speed with the day's experiences.

Susannah wondered why on earth Kirstin was thinking about Max Tarrant at all, considering what he'd done to her and was quite exasperated that she was giving him any airtime. Kirstin of course knew she was right, but she tried to explain it was like her mind was haunted with memories of what could have been, despite his continuous deception. Short of being exorcised, purportedly evicting this demon that possessed her mind, what else could she do?

She had been married to Max for 10 years, which wasn't that long, but the relationship developed when Kirstin was 14 and Max was 16 and that was highly significant, in that these were formative years, where she was trying to make sense of the world and where she might feature in it and in what capacity. It is where views, opinions, values are established and influenced and that was the dangerous part for Kirstin, looking back. She was a carefree, sensitive girl but too 'nice' to the point of naivety when it came to someone she cared about. He was the love of her life, the solver of all problems and yes, she had put him on a pedestal but for all the reasons that were now flawed and unforgivable.

Greg came downstairs, his hair still slightly wet but ready at least, as the taxi was beeping outside the front door. They arrived at the bohemian venue,

'Annie's' on White Hart Lane, around 8 o'clock and were shown into a softly-lit conservatory area, which was decorated with lanterns and beautiful flower arrangements. There was a cosy atmosphere all around and the place appeared full, which was a good sign. They were guided to a table in the far corner, conveniently away from other tables, and settled to enjoy the very pleasant ambiance and forthcoming British Mediterranean food that both Greg and Susannah had been praising to the hilt in the taxi.

The next morning Kirstin and Susannah took it easy, as they didn't have to be at London Gatwick until the early evening. Greg was working, so had already left and said his farewells at around 8.00 a.m. Susannah was still upstairs drying her hair and Kirstin was in the kitchen and had just started to make some scrambled eggs for them both for breakfast. The TV was on in the kitchen and the breakfast channel was in full flow with snippets of news and weather, celebrity interviews and the usual political theme of the moment under discussion. Suddenly, there was an interruption to the broadcast and the commentator indicated there was some breaking news. Kirstin stopped momentarily from stirring the scrambled eggs and listened more intently, as she wondered if it might be something that could possibly affect their flight to Monaco that evening. News flashes now were scary with hijacks, terrorists' attacks, impromptu strikes, walkouts or sudden celebrity deaths, all of which she didn't want to hear about now.

She stood motionless, staring at the screen and observed the scene that was being shown which was in Monte Carlo. Kirstin and Susannah were to visit the area of Monte Carlo during their stay in Monaco. It is just a short distance away and the two women had thought this would make an excellent evening trip to a top-class casino.

At that point Susannah entered the kitchen, looking bright-eyed, alert and wanting to know what she was staring at. Kirstin quickly pointed out it was about something that had happened in Monte Carlo and since they would shortly be on their way in that direction, she was trying to ascertain what exactly had happened.

It turned out that in one of the most luxurious casinos in Monte Carlo, the name of which had not been divulged in the news bulletin, there had been a shooting incident where several people had been injured, fortunately nobody had been killed but a well-known celebrity was amongst those injured, so this had warranted the high-profile news item to be broadcast as a breaking news debut.

Although somewhat alarmed to hear this news from the very location Kirstin and Susannah would soon be visiting, both women managed to sit and eat their scrambled eggs with not too much concern. Both decided to carry on with what was intended and not to let it spoil this soon to be tested, once in a lifetime experience.

They boarded the plane at London Gatwick at 6.00 p.m. and were flying direct to Nice, where they had booked a taxi to take them up the coast approximately 20 miles to Monaco, which would take about 20-25 minutes they had been informed. The flight was around two hours, so they were hoping for an estimated time of arrival at the Monte Carlo Bay Hotel, Av. Princess Grace, Monaco, of around 8.30 p.m.

Timings went to plan and as they drew nearer to their destination, the taxi driver indicated their hotel in the distance by flapping his hand in the air and shouting '*d'hôtel*'. It was dark but the hotel was grandly lit and stood majestically on rocks by the bay. There were palm trees gently swaying outside the magnificent entrance and curved steps leading up to the main doors. Once out of the taxi, it was possible to see the two-tone pink opulent building in more detail, with its arch-shaped windows and sweeping views of the beach. The legendary hotel had an ambience of chic sophistication and an aura of festivity all rolled into one.

Kirstin and Susannah couldn't wait to get inside.

Chapter 2

Phillip Alexander-Browne was sitting at the kitchen table of 18 Henshaw Gardens, which was a large semi-detached Victorian town house situated on the south side of Harrogate. He was sipping and blowing on a very hot cup of coffee, which he liked black, consequently steaming up his reading glasses. The whole kitchen had a heady aroma of freshly-ground coffee beans, which created a feeling of cosiness and tranquillity. The sun streamed through the huge sash windows which overlooked the enormous and immaculately manicured back garden. Running along the top of the windows was a beautiful stained-glass section, which, because of the sun, was sending out brilliant shards of coloured lights just like an iridescent rainbow on to the far wall.

Phil had found a brilliant gardener to keep both

the front and back gardens in near perfect condition throughout the year, as he and Kirstin were always working, so unable to keep on top of it themselves. Neither of them was particularly green-fingered but Kirstin did enjoy sitting and reading out there in the warmer weather.

Phil was relaxing, elbows on the table and engrossed in reading Saturday's Yorkshire Post. He had been married to Kirstin for 25 years and was five years her junior, which Kirstin loved as she flirtatiously called him her 'toy boy' whenever there was an opportunity. Kirstin refused to have the married name of Browne, even if it did have a rather unusual 'e' on the end. She wanted to keep her maiden name of Alexander, so it was decided it would be 'Kirstin and Phillip Alexander-Browne', a bit of a mouth full but she didn't care, it had a sort of noble sound about it she thought.

Just as he'd managed to take a decent gulp of coffee now it had cooled, his mobile phone gave its usual ping sound when it had received a text message. He stretched across the table to reach it and glanced quickly at the message. It was from Kirstin. He swiped his finger across his phone so opening the message fully.

It read – *Journey brilliant, hotel super chic, Monaco beyond belief, well the small part we've seen so far. Exclusive shopping trip today, I won't go too mad and casino experience tonight. Could win a fortune! Hope all is well. Love you. X*

Phil smiled to himself and was pleased they were both having a good time.

He sent a brief message back – *Enjoy!!!!! Speak soon. X*

*

Kirstin sighed. *A man of few words as usual,* she thought, snapping shut her phone case and turning to Susannah, who was also finishing her text messaging to Greg.

They were sat in the Blue Bay restaurant facing the sea and had just collected the start of their buffet breakfast. Susannah confirmed that Greg was fine and was eating out over the weekend. On Friday evening at Abbie's, their younger daughter of 30, and with James, their elder son of 35, on Saturday evening. They were both married and had small children, so Greg and Susannah were in effect grandparents, although had never married.

Susannah had shown Kirstin some photographs on the plane of the grandchildren and it was evident both Susannah and Greg were thrilled to bits with their arrival and all their developmental milestones, crawling, walking, talking etc. Susannah's phone was full to overflowing with photos.

Kirstin asked if Greg had made any more

comments about getting married, as he had always been of the opinion that they didn't need to. Greg had said nothing would be any different, only Susannah's surname and that she would wear a wedding ring. He of course wouldn't because he didn't like rings. He thought there was little point. Kirstin had thought this was a bit of a 'male chauvinist pig' attitude but hadn't ever conveyed this to Susannah.

Susannah had a feeling that now they had four very young grandchildren, Greg would do the honourable thing and succumb to a proper marriage service, exactly when she had no idea but hoped that Greg would surprise her. He had mellowed over the years and had recently hinted this may be a good thing to do and it would be a lovely family affair for everyone.

Kirstin smiled at her and hoped this would happen very soon. She felt upset for Susannah, who had always supported Greg in his work and brought up two children single-handed due to his many trips abroad and travelling around the country, which was part of his job at times.

Whilst they continued to eat their breakfast, Kirstin's mind was drawn back to the day she first found out she was pregnant. She was 19 and at University in London. Yes, it was Max Tarrant's and how it happened was a miracle. She was on the pill at the time, so it didn't make any sense, but what to do was the biggest dilemma ever. It wasn't to Kirstin, but it certainly was for Max. She had always dreamed as a young child that when this happened to her, she would be so thrilled and when the moment came to tell her husband, he would be over the moon and ecstatic with joy. What happened was so far from that dream. It was simply a case of 'you must organise an abortion.' Not even 'we', not that this was any consolation anyway, but it highlighted very clearly a despicable side of Max Tarrant. At that point in her life she had been with him for five years. It obviously meant very little.

Kirstin's Guardian Angel must have decided to take charge and thankfully for her, she had a miscarriage naturally. This obviously wasn't a good thing to happen to anyone but with hindsight now, it was probably for the best for Kirstin at the time. She could not have lived with the idea of having an abortion, not ever.

To further compound Kirstin's sadness and loss at this dreadful time, when she came out of hospital and returned to their flat, Max had been seeing and sleeping with someone else.

Was this naivety or adoration? Kirstin had known over those five years that there had been other such incidents. 'A leopard doesn't change its spots', but she wouldn't give up on this one, time and time again.

She often wondered why not.

Kirstin and Susannah left the Hotel in a black Mercedes that was dutifully waiting for them at the main entrance, ready to drop them off at the Le Metropole Shopping Centre where they were to start their shopping experience. Afterwards, they would move on to The Monte-Carlo Pavilions, a new shopping experience in the Boulingrins Gardens. The Hotel had recommended these places so they had been well informed of what to expect. High quality goods for high prices was what they were expecting but it would be an experience and they both loved people watching.

Le Metropole Shopping Centre was spectacular. It was facing the Casino Gardens and had around 80 boutiques. The ornate marble floors welcomed them beneath magnificent chandeliers. The whole inside was lavishly decorated with ornate ceilings and marble steps with very decorative wrought-iron balustrades and broad oak banisters.

After a couple of hours Kirstin and Susannah decided to give the Monte-Carlo Pavilions a miss. They became so engrossed with Le Metropole, they couldn't entice themselves away and it was very easy shopping just moving from one boutique to the next. They decided they would have lunch at some point and finish the day there eventually.

*

Back in Harrogate, Phil Alexander-Browne had planned to go up to the golf club for an afternoon's golf with a colleague. Phil was an accountant and now worked for a company in Harrogate having spent most of his working life in London, with Ernst & Young. He had been previously married and had, at the time, two young boys. His wife had met someone else, another woman, with whom she moved in with and took the boys with her. This was a very difficult time for Phil, who found the whole concept extremely hard to come to terms with. He was particularly concerned for his two young boys but in fact they seemed to settle and were in the end quite happy with this arrangement. Phil saw them regularly and they had holidays with him, as and when they could. Unfortunately, Phil was paying two mortgages and maintenance to his ex-wife for her and the boys, so there were several years of being hard-up.

He met Kirstin a year later, at a colleague's house party and they immediately bonded, recognising a friendship and closeness that neither of them had experienced for a long time.

They married three years later when Kirstin was 35 and Phil was 30. They both lived in London and decided to still reside there, so sold off one of their flats, which helped financially for a while. They were both earning reasonable money, Phil as an

Accountant and Kirstin as a University Lecturer, but living in London was costly and, with Phil's other commitments, this was sometimes very limiting as to what they could do together. Meals out, theatre trips and holidays had to be worked into a tight budget or had to be ruled out altogether.

Kirstin had bought Max out of their flat and having no offspring meant her commitments were quite different to those of Phil's.

*

Kirstin and Susannah arrived back at Monte Carlo Bay Hotel just after 6 p.m. They were both carrying several designer bags and were laughing uncontrollably as they entered the hotel reception. They'd had the most brilliant day and somehow managed to find a few sale items amongst all the rich and splendour of the Metropole Shopping Centre. They decided to call into the Blue Gin bar, with its beautiful terrace and view of the sea, for a special cocktail. They could relax for a while before they glammed up for their evening trip to the Casino de Monte-Carlo.

They found a comfortable space to sit and put down all their prize bargains and packages from the day's shopping trip by the side of the table. An American lady sitting close by commented on their array of bags and laughed saying they must have had one hell of a day. A typical American phrase but it had been one hell of a day.

She asked if Kirstin and Susannah had hit the Casinos yet and said she had been in the Casino de Monte-Carlo in the early hours of Friday morning, where there was some sort of gun battle going on. She and her husband were absolutely terrified, so they took refuge in a cleaning cupboard they happened to find open just by chance. Everyone was running for their lives and several people were seriously injured. The American lady was called Gladys and she continued to talk about the event, although by now Kirstin and Susannah had stopped listening.

Neither Kirstin nor Susannah could answer, as they had heard about this on Breakfast TV before they flew to Nice on that same Friday evening. They were stunned that they were going tonight to the very Casino where this had happened.

Just as Gladys had paused for breath, Kirstin quickly asked her if she knew what it was all about and who was the celebrity that was injured. Gladys waved an arm frantically in the air to someone over the far side of the bar and shouted 'Jack' half a dozen times before she got a response. A silver-haired, aristocratic-looking gentleman put up his hand and romped over to Gladys in a very athletic manner, suggesting he was quite fit. He was tall, rather distinguished-looking and had the same American drawl as Gladys, which can so easily grate after a while.

Gladys brought Jack up to speed by introducing Kirstin and Susannah to him before launching into their horrendous experience again at the Casino de Monte-Carlo. She finally reached the point where she said that they had been told that four masked men had entered the building through a delivery back door. They had guns but were clearly looking for someone as they weren't initially firing randomly. However, someone's bodyguard let rip and consequently, all hell let loose with security guards entering the mix too. Gladys looked at Jack and asked if he could remember the name of the celebrity who was injured. Jack laughed and conveyed that whoever this so-called celebrity was, he only had a small cut on his forehead, where he'd fallen over in his rush to escape and hit his head on the side of a table. It was only a scratch really, nothing more.

'What was his name?' Gladys insisted, irritated that Jack was now starting to ramble. Jack laughed again and said, 'Well if it means anything to you but it didn't to us, it was Max Tarrant.'

Chapter 3

Max Tarrant came from humble beginnings. His father worked in the steel industry all his life in Rotherham, and his mother worked in a large typing pool, in Mexborough, a short bus ride away. There was little money and times were hard. They lived just outside Rotherham in a village called Rawmarsh. His grandfather had worked all his life down the mines at Maltby Main Colliery, which closed many years ago. He struggled badly with poor health and died at 62. His grandmother was a cleaner at the local swimming baths for several years but had to give up in her fifties due to mobility problems. She died at 64, just two years after her husband. She couldn't manage on her own. Max's parents both died within a few years of each other around 30 years ago. Max was their only child, so inherited what little money there was but it was enough to put a deposit down on a small house for him and Kirstin back in 1973.

*

Kirstin and Susannah were still sat in the Blue Gin bar trying desperately to digest the news conveyed by Gladys and Jack. What they couldn't grasp was how could Max Tarrant be classed as a celebrity. Kirstin hadn't heard anything about him for at least 30 years, so she supposed anything might be possible. He did love the limelight and was certainly arrogant enough to carry off a celebrity status.

They were now running short of time and needed to get ready for their glamorous evening trip to the Casino de Monte-Carlo. Just as they were heading in the direction of the lift, Susannah suddenly had a brainwave and suggested that as soon as they got back tonight that they Google Mr Tarrant, to see exactly what he's up to. This made Kirstin hoot with laugher, as Susannah was the last person to be interested in Max Tarrant, but she secretly thought it was a good idea.

The taxi arrived on the dot of 8 p.m. and both Kirstin and Susannah looked stunning. Kirstin wore a soft pastel pink chiffon dress, which was virtually backless but so elegant. Her shoes and clutch bag were bought in the morning's shopping spree and had been a bargain. They were nude in colour and a shiny patent leather. The whole outfit looked perfect with Kirstin's naturally blonde hair, green eyes and olive skin colour.

Susannah's outfit was similar in that it also was of soft see-through chiffon but was a two-piece consisting of top and wide floaty trousers. The top had some small sequin flowers, which caught the light beautifully, and a fine camisole underneath. It was in a shade of Mediterranean green, which suited Susannah's dark brown hair, brown eyes and dark skin tone. Susannah had also bought the same shoes and clutch bag as Kirstin but in a gold colour.

The taxi took about 10 minutes to the Casino de Monte-Carlo. It was much nearer than Kirstin and Susannah had anticipated, and they were delighted to arrive so quickly.

They were both in awe of this magnificent and imposing building. It overlooked the Mediterranean Sea and was built in 1863 by a famous architect called Charles Garnier.

As the taxi pulled up at the main entrance, alongside three huge oak doors, a sparkling circular fountain could be seen in front of the building which added to its majestic charm. It glittered dramatically in the lights and created an ambience of glitzy glamour. A uniformed doorman rushed to open the taxi door and formally ushered Kirstin and Susannah through the huge doors, where they were met with a sensational sight of enormous Bohemian glass chandeliers, rococo ceilings and a columned gold and marble atrium. Both women stood transfixed. This building had more than a WOW factor and they just couldn't take in all the surrounding splendour.

The Casino de Monte-Carlo offered all the services and amenities that you could possibly desire. Their Hotel had booked dinner for them at the Le Salon Rose restaurant. They had described it as a high-end brassiere-style restaurant with Mediterranean-inspired cuisine. A table had been booked on the terrace which overlooked the sea. How perfect was that?

Kirstin and Susannah were ushered in the direction of the Le Salon Rose and were warmly greeted by the very smartly dressed Restaurant Manager, who asked whose name the table was booked under. Kirstin confirmed it was hers and they were led directly to the very spacious and opulent terrace.

They were led to the far end of the terrace, where the table was screened on two sides by tall floaty foliage, planted in enormous ornamental pots. The terrace area was extremely busy, and they were pleased to be placed out of the main hustle and bustle of it.

They were handed the menus and spent some time deciding on what to have. The menu was extensive, and it was hard to make their final choices when the young Italian waiter returned.

Finally, Kirstin chose 'Crab and Avocado Tartare, Exotic Salad and Citrus Vinaigrette' for her starter followed by 'Sea Bass Fillet served with a Canaille tomato, red pepper and garlic sauce'. Susannah was still desperately trying to decide but eventually went for the 'Salmon marinated in mild spices, asparagus and lemon cream sauce', followed by 'John Dory Supreme with artichokes, confit potatoes and olives'. It all sounded wonderful.

They ordered a bottle of Chateau Vaudois 'Valdes' 2014 French Rosé and some sparkling water, which arrived within minutes at their table in a large wine casket filled with ice. The waiter poured their drinks and the women clinked their glasses together and sipped the chilled Rosé, delighting in how relaxing and luxurious it all was. The view of the sea was spectacular and the glimmering night lights and selection of candles all around added to the sumptuous atmosphere.

Just as they were settling into a conversation about their shopping experiences earlier that day, Susannah's gold evening bag started shuddering and moving towards the edge of the table. It was her mobile phone vibrating and Susannah stared at it with concern, as she just couldn't imagine who would be phoning her apart from Greg but thought this was unlikely unless it was an emergency. She grabbed the bag and wrenched out her mobile phone. She glanced at the contact and mouthed 'oh no!' under her breath. Susannah excused herself from the table and walked over to a quiet area of the terrace. Kirstin was a bit worried, as she assumed it was Greg with some sort of problem but then thought he wouldn't be phoning her at this moment, knowing the agenda. Plus, she was sure they had already spoken to each other that morning.

Susannah was some time but luckily arrived back at the table just as the starters were being served. She was flustered and her face was a delicate shade of pink, spreading like a fan down her neck and onto her chest.

'I'm so sorry about that, Kirstin,' she spluttered. 'Let's just eat this and I will explain.'

Susannah fanned herself with the large soft white cotton serviette, at the same time as taking a large gulp of the Rosé wine, to try and calm herself down.

Kirstin said very little to Susannah whilst they were eating, as she could see how shaken she was and just wanted her to slowly relax and calm herself, without any questioning at all. Visibly Susannah returned to her normal colouring and the tension held in her shoulders relaxed back down.

'That was Celia, Celia Harrison. Do you remember her, Kirstin?'

'Umm, not sure really. Was she the one who came to your New Year's Eve party, with that rather strange husband?'

'Yes, yes, that's the one,' replied Susannah hurriedly, eager to move on with the story.

'Well, her rather strange husband as you put it, has just locked her in the house and taken all the keys. He says he wants to keep her safe, as there have been several burglaries lately in their area, so while he goes to the gym for an hour, she's locked up. She's beside herself and can't get out of a window either, as he has all the window lock keys.'

The waiter returned to clear their plates, which interrupted Kirstin's response. He asked if everything had been all right. Both women nodded their heads in unison and thanked him profusely for the excellent starters, in rather a hurried matter-of-fact way so they could move on, but they genuinely meant it.

'Oh, how ridiculous!' retorted Kirstin, frustrated by the stupidity of the incident. 'What if there's a fire? She won't be safe then! Is she calling the police or someone to help her? Why you, Susannah, you can't do anything from over here?'

Susannah shook her head and explained Celia's family lived some distance away and that her husband Ray didn't care for them or want Celia to be too involved with them. He said they constantly put her down and undermined her ability.

There had been quite a few incidents over the years Susannah had known Celia, where Ray, in her view, was overpowering and manipulative.

Their main courses arrived; they looked divine. The presentation of both dishes was just exquisite. How were they ever going to readjust to life once removed from this beautiful place?

The women tucked into their meal and continued to discuss Celia's situation, which Susannah said was a form of domestic abuse known as 'Coercive Control'. She had read about it in a magazine and was sure this was what was going on. Susannah had advised Celia to try and organise a counsellor for herself without Ray knowing if she could, as she needed serious help.

Kirstin agreed but then let the subject drop. She continued quietly with her meal. Deep in thought, she had returned to her 19-year-old self and remembered the trauma of miscarrying her baby and returning to Max to find out he had been living and sleeping with someone else, whilst she was in hospital. It was bizarre the way he had greeted her home, so pleased to see her. He told her everything and then produced a handmade crocheted gilet from the women he'd been with, as a gift. How could anyone do that? More concerning and difficult to comprehend now, was why she had ever stayed with him.

A few years later, when she was married to Max and moved to live in Amsterdam with him, she reflected how she had arrived with all their possessions from the UK and was so excited to be starting a new life together, suddenly to discover in their new apartment, an intimate and detailed letter from a woman who had been living with him over the last 6 months. It was earth-shattering, humiliating, cruel and unforgiving. Max told her it meant nothing of course and that he had been bored and lonely without her. He insisted it was only her he wanted, and it had just been a fling.

Kirstin stared at her empty plate and could feel the sting of tears in her eyes that would fall at any moment unless she pulled herself together quickly.

'Are you all right, Kirstin?' Susannah suddenly asked having just finished her meal too. 'You've been deep in thought.'

'Oh, was I, yes, I'm absolutely fine, just thinking about how much I might win on the roulette table tonight and what my tactics are going to be,' she chortled.

The waiter arrived to clear their plates. They had decided to abstain from desserts in preference to finishing off the Rosé wine and just watch the gentle lapping of the sea on the impeccable white sand.

Both women stared out to sea, both with their

own thoughts. Susannah was still thinking about Celia and hoped she would be all right. Kirstin, well, she had drifted back to the past and as thoughts whizzed through her head, she began to recognise that she had been a victim of coercive control too.

Chapter 4

After visiting the ladies' room and checking on their hair and makeup, Kirstin and Susannah headed in the direction of the gaming rooms and bars. The Casino is truly an iconic, awesome and mesmerising place. With its beautiful ornate Beaux Arts architecture and lavish décor, the interior of paintings and sculptures encapsulates an atmosphere of high energy and opulence. Such extravagance is magical to its clientele, who sometimes cannot resist its charms. There are several private lounges and bars available for high-rollers, who have succumbed to its temptations. The game will never let you go.

Kirstin and Susannah had read up all about the Casino prior to their trip and wanted desperately to witness what had inspired Ian Fleming's first novel 'Casino Royale', he was so taken with its splendour.

The Casino Monte Carlo also featured in his portrayals of 'Never Say Never Again' and 'Golden Eye'.

The women hadn't realised that photography was strictly forbidden inside the Casino's gilded rooms, something that the Hotel reception had mentioned to them before leaving. They were also reassured there would be no trouble of any sort, as the Casino has a zero-tolerance environment. This was slightly amusing considering the episode that happened last week involving Max Tarrant. What was surprising were the hundreds of people employed at the Casino to keep the place meticulous, from the valet parking staff to the craftsmen who construct and maintain the gambling tables. There is even a special stock room to house 36,000 packs of cards, which must be kept at 20 degrees centigrade!

There are many sectors within the Casino de Monte Carlo that require a high level of staffing to function effectively, efficiently and securely, in this intrinsically fabulous place. Therefore, reliable and trustworthy staffing is paramount.

There can be no compromising of gambling results. This is a private world of codes and unconventional behaviour.

Kirstin and Susannah ordered themselves a couple of gin and tonics at the bar and drifted over to a space where they could see Gladys and Jack talking to a small group of people. Gladys and Jack were delighted to see Kirstin and Susannah and quickly introduced them to those in the gathering. It became clear that most of the group were guests from the same hotel, Monte Carlo Bay. They all chatted for quite a while, mainly about the incident that occurred at the Casino the previous week. One or two of the guests had been there too, just like Gladys and Jack.

Kirstin spoke with a very dignified-looking man, with jet-black hair, which was so obviously dyed and far from realistic. His furrowed brow and many wrinkles suggested he was certainly in his late sixties, probably older. However, he was pleasant enough and was from California and on holiday with his wife. His name was Ed, and his wife was called Felicity, she was from England but had lived in America for over 30 years. She was quite glamorous, with soft blonde hair, cut into a neat bob, which framed her elfin-shaped face. She was wearing some very expensive-looking jewellery, which continually caught the light, reflecting sparkles everywhere, making an impressive statement.

The couple were saying how very odd the whole situation had been last week, as it seemed to happen so quickly. One minute everyone was enjoying themselves and suddenly there were people flying everywhere, particularly once the firing started. It was almost as if the four masked men had literally just walked in without being challenged in any way, which seemed highly unlikely given the extreme level of security, clearly visible everywhere.

Casino de Monte Carlo compliments itself on its high security standards. Most staff have worked there for many years and are respected for their loyalty, reliability and trustworthiness. Ed and Felicity expressed concern, as all did not seem normal that night. There were apparently some unanswered questions regarding the terrorists' entry and exit. This was communicated by one of the Gaming Room Managers, who had led Ed and Felicity to a safe place that night. He disclosed this information to Ed and Felicity, when he recognised them this evening and came over to see how they were now.

They all decided they probably would never know the true outcome and concluded their conversation by moving on to play a little roulette and the slot machines.

Kirstin and Susannah went over to the slot machines, although neither was concentrating, their minds still wondering what was behind all this. The police were continuing to take statements and investigating the matter, but nothing was seemingly heading towards a conclusion of any sort.

As Susannah was reaching for her clutch bag, which she'd placed on the floor by a slot machine, a woman rushing, half running, knocked her off balance. Susannah was suddenly a heap on the floor and was semi-dazed. The woman who was in staff uniform immediately stopped and helped Susannah to her feet. She was apologising profusely and appeared flustered and anxious. Susannah reassured her she was fine, as by now several other members of staff had congregated to give assistance and it was attracting too much attention for Susannah's liking.

Susannah conveyed she was fine, and the fuss and the staff disseminated.

Shortly afterwards, the woman who had knocked Susannah over appeared by her side with an ornate gold tray, with two rather expensive-looking cocktails balanced. She said she hoped she hadn't spoilt their evening and the cocktails were for them to enjoy, with her compliments.

This was all very lovely and both Kirstin and Susannah settled in to some serious gambling.

They had both won small amounts on the various slot machines and were having fun. They decided to try their luck on a nearby roulette table. As they were moving across to take their seats, Kirstin caught a glimpse of the woman who had created the collision with Susannah earlier. She was quite a distance over the other side of the Casino, but she was chatting enthusiastically with a customer. She saw her give him a small piece of paper, which he immediately put in his pocket. The woman then sidled away surreptitiously and through a door for staff only. This was probably a purely innocent situation, but the observation stuck in Kirstin's mind for a moment.

The roulette table was now full and chips were being bestowed like falling confetti, virtually covering the green-biased table. The wheel-spinning at this table went on for some time before Kirstin and Susannah decided to finally call it a day and order a taxi. They had both won some and lost some but mainly broken even with their finances. It had all been an experience and good fun.

The two women moved from the table and went to say goodnight to Gladys, Jack, Ed and Felicity, who were now having coffee and liqueurs. They chatted briefly about their flutters on the tables and slot machines and bid them goodnight. They would probably see them at breakfast tomorrow.

As the women were heading towards the main door for the doorman to call a taxi, a tall man in a suit approached them. He was obviously staff and had a badge, which indicated he was a Casino Room Manager. He said it had come to his attention that Susannah had been knocked over and wanted to apologise and make sure she was not injured in any way. Susannah reaffirmed she was fine. It was just a bit of a shock at the time, that was all. The man, whose name was Ricardo Lucca, put his hand inside his jacket pocket and pulled out an envelope in which he said there were two complimentary tickets to dine in the Le Salon Rose at their convenience. He apologised again and hoped to see them again soon. He led the way to the main door and instructed the doorman to call a taxi back to The Monte Carlo Bay Hotel.

Kirstin and Susannah were taken by surprise by this gesture and for a moment or two could not respond. They eventually managed to thank Ricardo Lucca but weren't entirely sure how this very generous gesture had come about exactly, or indeed why? Was this the Casino's usual practice, when such a low-level incident occurred? This incident had already been honoured by the complimentary cocktails anyway. Puzzling as this was to appreciate, both Kirstin and Susannah were, at this moment in time, too weary to give any further thought to it.

The taxi was hailed by the doorman and both women slumped into the back of the sumptuous black leather seats of the silver Mercedes and sighed heavily. They closed their eyes and relaxed.

They arrived back at the Monte Carlo Bay Hotel around 2 a.m. There were few guests around and the mood was of tranquillity and peace. This immediately initiated the feeling of sleep. Kirstin and Susannah said their goodnights and went up to their rooms, arranging to meet up at breakfast around 10 a.m.

Kirstin lay motionless in her bed. It was extremely dark now she had turned off the small dimmed lamp at her bedside. Only a faint glimmer of light had smuggled its way under the main door. It was 3 a.m. and silent. Her mind kept straying, preventing sleep. She was exhausted and tried desperately to blank her thoughts.

'Coercive control' was now in her head. Kirstin had never heard of this term until this evening, or rather last night considering the time now. Susannah had defined it in detail, when she explained a close friend's current situation, regarding the relationship with her husband. Much of what was said very much resonated with Kirstin's past life and provided reasons as to why the woman she once was had slowly vanished over the years.

At some point after this consideration, Kirstin fell into a deep sleep. Her mind continued to wander, and in its usual pattern of events, focused on her early life as a young girl. This was a recurring stream of thoughts and reflections that were never far away from the surface of her subconscious mind.

Reflection is a strange thing. It does not always serve a useful purpose.

Chapter 5

Back in Barnes, London, Greg was preparing a meal. Since Kirstin's and Susannah's departure, Greg had been having quite a sociable time. His two grown-up children, Abbie and James, had invited him over for meals on Friday and Saturday evening. Saturday, he did some food shopping and played squash with a friend and he intended to spend some time with work colleagues in the evenings next week, either having a drink or meal out and probably frequenting the gym. He certainly had it all worked out.

Tonight, he was preparing a meal for a previous colleague, who had moved to another newspaper some years ago. Greg had kept in regular contact with him. He too was an editorial producer like Greg, and they had been good sparring partners when they had worked together, each challenging the other, arguing and wrangling for top position.

Rob Harrison was a well-educated man, who was now in his late fifties. He had been married for several years but sadly this had come to an end when his wife had an affair and decided she was leaving him. They divorced and she remarried someone else. There were no children, but it all came as a devastating shock to Rob and for a long time he retreated into himself and lived a hermit's existence. Greg could see what was happening and started to invite him for a drink after work, to encourage him back into the social scene again. Rob was reluctant at first but was, after a time, grateful to Greg for breaking his lonely routine. Over time, Rob was welcomed at Greg and Susannah's home for meals and they all became good friends.

Tonight's meal was to be fresh prawns in garlic with smoked salmon, followed by fillet steak, mushrooms, asparagus and grilled tomatoes. Greg had bought a variety of good cheeses to round off with and had a bottle or two of Rioja lined up, as an accompaniment throughout the meal.

Greg had allowed himself loads of time to prepare everything and it certainly wasn't a complicated meal to produce, so he went for a shower and took his time getting changed and ready for his guest. Whilst in the shower, he was thinking about Susannah and whether she was having a good time. They had been in text contact since she had left, and all seemed to be going very well. Greg thought the change of scenery would do her good and spending time with Kirstin would allow her just to relax and not be at the family's beck and call, particularly now, with their four grandchildren.

Greg realised he hadn't been around much when their children were growing up and was aware that Susannah had borne the brunt of singlehandedly bringing them up alone. He couldn't believe where all the years had gone but was not regretful in any way, as he enjoyed his family and cared very much for Susannah.

Once he was finished showering, dried off and changed, Greg went to start the meal preparation. He poured himself a large glass of Pinot Grigio and set to work. Rob was due round at 8 p.m., which was another hour away, so plenty of time.

Rob was returning home from Barnes Squash Club having played with a work colleague. Greg had also started to play squash over the last year. He wasn't terribly sporty, but Rob had convinced him that it would be good exercise and worth a try. Amazingly enough, Greg adjusted incredibly quickly to this fast-paced sport and although initially, technically unfit he stuck with it and massively improved his stamina. Rob also introduced Greg to the Gym to do Circuit and Weight Training. This all worked out well and Greg felt invigorated and enthused by his new-found hobbies. Susannah wasn't particularly enamoured, as she was again alone but soon put herself out for hire for the grandchildren and was happy helping as much as she could.

It was five to eight. The doorbell rang at the charming, elegant and extremely spacious four bedroomed semi-detached Victorian house in Cleveland Road. The road was quiet and in the heart of Barnes near to the village green, Barnes pond and an eclectic mixture of shops. Susannah and Greg had lived here for around 25 years and they had seen a massive rise in property prices. Their home now was worth over two million pounds, which they found quite unbelievable.

Greg hurried to the door to greet his guest and hugged Rob on entering the hallway. He patted him cheerfully on the back whilst accepting a bottle of Bollinger Champagne swaddled in crisp white tissue paper which Rob was clutching close to his chest. Both men strolled through the large double reception area to the kitchen positioned at the back of the house. There was a large Marston & Langinger conservatory adjoining the kitchen, which served as a dining room. It was exquisite, painted in a soft pale green, which brought warmth to the whole area. This led onto a stunning courtyard with a feature water fountain.

Susannah loved the garden and everything in it had to be just perfect. The garden was south facing, so was beautiful in the summer for barbecues and entertaining friends. It was also wonderful for just sitting and relaxing under the pergola, appreciating nature, reading or drifting off and dreaming.

Rob made himself comfortable on a high black leather stool situated by the central marble-topped island. Greg grabbed two champagne glasses from a nearby glass-fronted unit and popped open the Bollinger. It was icy cold, as Rob had the foresight to have put it briefly in the freezer before leaving home.

The two men clinked their glasses and sat together whilst savouring their champagne and hand-cooked Tyrrells lightly sea-salted crisps. They talked for some time about business and colleagues they both knew, before sitting at the dining table and starting their meal.

Greg was quite well-housetrained regarding entertaining and had lit candles and dimmed lights to create ambiance and relaxation. Not that this was to create a romantic setting, but more of an unwind and chill setting.

Rob and Greg spent a couple of hours enjoying their meal and later retired to the living room with a large glass of Rioja each. It had been an excellent evening and both men were very relaxed in each other's company.

Rob enquired about Susannah and how the trip to Monaco was going and queried if Greg was having difficulty fending for himself. Greg was someone who did, on occasions, enjoy his own company but had missed there being no one to come home to and the quiet undisturbed feel of the house, nothing had moved or altered since leaving in the early morning.

Rob understood this, as he experienced these feelings every day. His own company was something he hated and, although working all day, some weekends and evenings had become desperately lonely. Greg saw Rob regularly at least twice a week, so was surprised by these comments, as he did have other friends too. Rob explained that it was about not being attached to anyone, not being an item where you spend quality time with someone. Greg asked if he had thought about trying a dating agency or something similar. Rob disclosed this was not his scene at all and did not want the hassle of joining something he referred to as an online cattle market. Greg found that quite amusing and chuckled to himself as he pictured it in his mind.

It was approaching midnight and both men were working in the morning, so decided to call it a day. Rob lived over the other side of the village green about fifteen, twenty minutes' walk away, so it would not take him long. He preferred to walk instead of taking a cab, as the fresh air would do him good, he decided.

Greg led the way back through to the front door and turned to Rob, handing him his jacket. Without hesitation, Rob leaned forward taking his jacket with one hand and placed his other hand on Greg's shoulder, pulling him sharply towards him. He kissed Greg passionately on the lips and surprisingly Greg did not pull away from this but instead responded, as though it was a usual and familiar action. This scene lasted only a few seconds but seemed like it had happened in slow motion and had now paused. Rob threw his jacket to the floor and hugged Greg with all his strength but was sobbing uncontrollably. Greg comforted his friend and led him back into the living room, where they sat together for a while on the soft cream leather sofa.

Greg went to get two glasses of Glenmorangie and ice, so they could talk about what had just taken place. Rob had calmed himself but looked like he needed a drink. Greg returned with the drinks and handed one to Rob. He sat beside him again and put a comforting arm around his shoulder. He asked what this was all about, although he already knew.

For many years, Greg had questioned his sexuality, even as far back as a teenager. He had many close friends of both sexes but had, over the years, felt an attraction to certain male friends but had never voiced his feelings openly or discussed this with anyone. These were not attractions exclusive to men only, he sometimes was very attracted to certain women too. However, he felt deep down that this was why he had a resistance to marriage and why he had evaded it all these years with Susannah. He cared very much for Susannah but whether this was ever love he couldn't be sure. Was it friendship, companionship, a convenience or had he adjusted to this way of living? His head was full of questions and he felt unnerved and slightly shaken by his reactions.

Rob was initially silent and slowly sipped his whisky. He put his hand gently on Greg's knee. Greg responded by placing his hand over his and reassuringly patted it gently. The two men remained in silence for a few minutes and took stock of what this meant and what the implications were, if any.

Greg finally asked Rob how long he had felt this way or was it a totally spontaneous reaction. Rob explained he had felt like it for some time but hadn't wanted to admit his attraction and had felt foolish and embarrassed by his feelings.

After a while Rob suggested he should go and to discuss this at another time when they were fresh and analyse it all in the cool light of day. Rob stood up and collected his jacket. Greg walked him slowly to the front door, with his arm around his shoulders. He continued to reaffirm his actions towards him had been reciprocated, confirming his feelings for Rob.

Rob was still quite tearful but didn't want to put any pressure on Greg to confirm or deny how he felt about him until they had a proper chat later.

Greg embraced Rob and hugged him tightly. This was not going to go away, and they were clearly very emotionally involved with each other. This was something that had suddenly erupted and unfolded. Their friendship was long and deep, so had these true feelings suddenly reached the surface?

Greg persuaded Rob to stay and not walk home, as he was too emotional and upset. It was not a good idea in the early hours to attempt to make his way home. Rob was initially resistant, saying he would be fine and that maybe they both needed a break away from each other to consider their actions.

Rob finally agreed. Between them they cleared up the remaining dinner crockery and glasses into the dish washer and both retreated upstairs to bed.

As Greg put his head down on the pillow, he heard the distinctive ping of his mobile phone. He went over to the chest of drawers where his mobile brightly displayed a message.

He swiped his finger across to read the message in full. It read: -

Hi Darling,

What an evening we had on Saturday! Absolutely,

fabulous! Today quite intriguing! Something exciting seems to be happening every day. Missing you lots though. Hope everything is okay and that you aren't too lonely. Love you! S xx

Greg stared at the message for a few seconds, his thoughts in tatters. He turned off the mobile and returned to bed where he realised Rob had dropped off to sleep.

Chapter 6

Kirstin sat at the breakfast table alone. She was down first, so had indicated to the waiter that she was waiting for her companion and would just have some coffee for now. She was early deliberately, as she wanted some time on her own. She wanted to get things straight in her head.

There were several thoughts that were bothering her. Last night for instance, why did Ricardo Lucca present them with two complimentary tickets to dine at the Le Salon Rose when they had already been given cocktails for the unfortunate incident where Susannah was knocked to the ground? It was a bit over the top. Secondly, what was going on with the waitress, when Kirstin saw her give a small piece of paper to a male customer, who hurriedly put it in his pocket and finally, what was Max Tarrant's true involvement in all this? There was more to it all and Kirstin was determined to find out. They were both extremely tired last night and neither had felt like Googling Max Tarrant but perhaps that's something they could do later today.

At that moment, Susannah arrived at the table apologising if she was a bit late. Kirstin said she wasn't, and the waiter promptly came over to ask if she would like tea or coffee. Susannah sat down and together they looked through the breakfast menu. They both finally decided on some cantaloupe melon slices followed by cheese omelette, mushrooms and tomatoes.

After exchanging how each other had slept, they discussed the evening at the Casino. Kirstin relayed all the oddities of the evening, leaving Susannah flummoxed, as she was unaware of the incident with the waitress giving the small piece of paper to a male customer. What on earth was that all about, she wondered but was it anything at all? It could just have been that he was asking for her mobile number. Perhaps he wanted to take her out. Who knows, but Susannah didn't think it was worth concerning themselves with.

Their breakfasts arrived and they spent the next half an hour talking over the evening, who'd they met, what was said and how fortunate they were at having another opportunity to dine at Le Salon Rose totally free of charge.

Just as the waiter was clearing the final plates from their table and pouring them additional coffee, Susannah's mobile rang. She quickly grabbed it from her bag and moved to a quiet place away from all the busyness of the breakfast area. She glanced back at Kirstin and mouthed it was Celia. Kirstin acknowledged and decided to sit and enjoy her coffee and check her phone for any messages or e-mails whilst Susannah was missing. *Heaven knows what's happened now*, she contemplated. Celia was not in a good place and Kirstin assumed the worst, as she was sure she wouldn't otherwise be phoning.

Kirstin flicked open her phone case and there as if by magic, a message just appeared. It was from Phil, it read: - *Hope all is going well with you two and you are enjoying yourselves. How was the Casino? Do you need to send a bank transfer over with all you've won? XX*

Kirstin smiled and wished she could text back that a few million was on its way. Sadly not, but it was good to hear from him and she spent a few minutes responding in brief of events to date. She checked out a few e-mails, snapped her phone shut and finished off her coffee.

She turned her gaze to a table that was partly screened by a large white pillar but where she had heard raised voices. She could see two men at the table and there was obviously another, whom they were talking to, whose identity was obscured by the pillar. One of the men she could see, but only from the back, suddenly pushed his chair back in an aggressive and angry manner and stormed out of the breakfast area. The other man she could see was now saying something to the person obscured by the pillar and he too walked out, but without all the dramatics of the first man. *How strange*, she thought, *what was going on there?* As she was about to look away and refocus on something else, the person behind the pillar was emerging. It was another man but this man Kirstin knew immediately. It was the person the waitress had given the piece of paper to last night. How very interesting was that.

Kirstin could see Susannah returning and poured her another coffee, as there was surely another problem looming with poor Celia and they needed to try and help her somehow.

'Oh, what a terrible mess, Kirstin,' Susannah started off. 'You'll never believe this.' Susannah explained that when Celia's husband Ray got back from the gym about an hour after he'd left, Celia had smashed a downstairs window at the back of the house and was just knocking out all the sharp pieces around the edge with a rolling pin, so she could safely climb out. At that point, Ray flew into the study, which was where Celia was, and immediately seeing the state of the window punched her in the face. Kirstin gasped and recoiled in horror at the thought of this terrible scene.

Susannah continued and said, 'It's all right Kirstin, Celia had the presence of mind to then lash out and the rolling pin was still in her hand, so she knocked him unconscious. Slightly humorous as this may sound, it was quite a serious incident and Celia was then beside herself with guilt and fear. She immediately phoned the ambulance and the police too. They arrived quickly and whilst they were there Ray started to come around, so she felt slightly better, but the ambulance still took Ray to hospital for checks. The police then took a statement from Celia, everything came out about what had been going on. They called someone to board-up the window for her and radioed to say there were taking Celia to stay with a family member for her own safety. The police would also be speaking to Ray at the hospital, as he had imprisoned and assaulted Celia and there would be serious consequences. They also gave Celia information as to where she could get some help and support and they would be informing her doctor. Celia was extremely upset and distraught by the whole thing but understood this was probably all for the best and agreed to everything.

Kirstin was flabbergasted when Susannah finally finished telling her the tale but was very pleased this was the outcome, of what was now a violent situation and one that Celia needed to be out of for her own good.

Kirstin went on to say that she too had been punched in the face by Max, as she was trying to leave him. Not exactly a good way to encourage someone to stay with you but it was the beginning of the end, so to speak. She had to wear dark glasses for a while at the University where she lectured, as she had a black eye but explained to others it was an eye infection she needed to keep covered. She also needed to be checked out at the dentist, as she had severe pain down the left side of her face affecting her teeth. The dentist had asked what happened, Kirstin told him a heavy suitcase had fallen out of a top cupboard, hitting her in the eye and face. The dentist didn't look too convinced but that was her story and she was sticking to it.

Kirstin recalled speaking to Max's father on the phone after this incident and he had said that she had probably asked for it. She was initially speechless by this deplorable comment but managed to respond by saying she knew where he'd got his bullying tactics from and put down the phone. That was the last time she spoke or heard from him again. Susannah was staring at her in disbelief. She had known about some of the antics of Mr Max Tarrant but not that he had resorted to violence towards Kirstin in any way.

Kirstin had touched on aspects of her life with Max with Susannah, but she had never gone into any real detail. They decided to move from the breakfast area and sit more comfortably on the nearby terrace by the pool and relax a little before deciding what they would do for the rest of the day.

Kirstin explained she was unaware of what coercive control was until Susannah had mentioned it, in relation to Celia, but was now convinced this was exactly what her situation had been with Max. Susannah looked a bit surprised by this, but Kirstin went on to verify it was something that had started early in their teenage years but that she hadn't taken it on board. If anything, she had viewed his behaviour as being caring and protective. Slowly over the years, things happened that were much more controlling. For instance, when they moved to Amsterdam, Max was desperate for her to become pregnant and forget about her career aspirations. He didn't like her regularly speaking to her family or going out too much with her friends. He restricted her money, saying just to let him know when she needed anything. The worst came when he cut up all her credit cards, so she couldn't leave and return to the UK. At that point she took an overdose and was hospitalised for a short period. Again, the usual scenario on her return home, she discovered he had been seeing someone else. Max had other women on a regular basis, but she knew that the final straw had come when he informed her that he was using and paying for prostitutes. She then ended up with a sexually transmitted disease, which took weeks of treatment to clear. On another day around this same time, she discovered a hand gun in their apartment and wondered what else was going on to warrant having a gun. 'There was no trust there anymore,' Kirstin sighed, 'I had to leave him forever.'

Susannah had listened to the detail of these past events and thought how remarkably stable Kirstin was considering all the traumatic times she had with Max Tarrant and indeed how she had ever coped with him for so long. Love is blind. She was his possession.

After a depressing hour of hearing about Celia and more of the same past events of Kirstin's life with Max, they decided to go and check him out on Google, as they meant to last night, to see what he was up to now and maybe why he was in Monaco last week.

Susannah had brought her iPad, so they both returned to her room. On the way, Kirstin suddenly saw the man she recognised at breakfast exiting a room just a few doors down from Susannah's room. He was too near for Kirstin to warn Susannah but ideal for Kirstin to get a much closer look at him. He was of Mediterranean appearance, with a swarthy complexion and was quite tall, over six foot and of a slim build. He walked past Susannah and Kirstin, without acknowledgement, his gaze dead ahead and his mind preoccupied.

Susannah swiped her door card in the lock and they both entered her room. As soon as the door was shut, Kirstin explained to Susannah what had happened at breakfast, whilst she was talking to Celia. Susannah didn't like the sound of this much and was even more concerned that his room was so close to hers, considering his dodginess so far. Kirstin reiterated that nothing had happened to cause concern, only a suspicion had occurred at the Casino that something seemed odd. Susannah agreed.

Susannah sought out her iPad and went to work on investigating what she could on Max Tarrant. It wasn't long before information about him was revealed, it was strange and didn't quite add up. All the searches revealed that he was now a Game Show Host, in New York. The two women were flabbergasted. This was the most unlikely area of entertainment that Max Tarrant could ever pull off. It was not his style or scene in anyway. There had to be something more to this story. Susannah and Kirstin were already viewing their findings as some sort of red herring or cover up. They pledged to make it their business to find out the truth.

Kirstin and Susannah decided they needed a little sightseeing and had the rest of the day left just to do that. They had already studied the various places that were a must to visit and had highlighted the Oceanographic Museum and Monaco Harbour. They opted for the Museum for this afternoon, as there was loads to see and do. They also rather liked the sound of having a relaxing drink later in the lounge at Turtle Island, located in the West Terrace of the Museum.

The women went down to reception and ordered a taxi. In seconds, it appeared, much to their surprise and delight. They asked the driver to take them to the Oceanographic Museum on Avenue Saint Martin. The Museum was just a stone's throw from the Prince's Palace and was a stunningly majestic piece of architecture, perched on the side of the cliffs of the Rock of Monaco. It rose out of the sea 85 metres high and had taken 11 years to build. A most impressive sight.

As the two women vacated the taxi, they could see lifts and escalators not too far ahead, which would lead them to the main entrance.

This was going to be an exciting afternoon. They were about to experience an incredible Marine adventure.

Chapter 7

Back in Kensington, London, Greg was sat at his desk in Northcliffe House, staring intently at his laptop screen. His thoughts were elsewhere, and it wasn't until his mobile vibrated violently that he reacted or became separated from his mind's confusion.

It was Monday morning and he had left Rob in bed. Greg needed to be in work earlier than usual. Rob hadn't woken, so it made it easier for Greg to just get ready and leave. He had left Rob a note in the kitchen next to the shiny chrome and copper Dualit kettle, explaining he would contact him later. He left home at 6.30 a.m. He hadn't bothered with any breakfast, preferring to pick up a coffee and something to eat on route. He just needed to remove himself from the house, as soon as possible. He needed space and time to think.

Sunday had become a dreamy mist of events, where he couldn't link one incident to another. As time passed, the situation seemed unreal and Greg even questioned if it had happened at all. His mind was mixed with so many emotions it created a block to think beyond, what next?

His attention was then taken by the message displayed on his phone. It read: - *Hi, Sorry I missed you. In work now too. A great evening! Thanks. Could we meet later? R x*

Greg slightly recoiled and pushed away the mobile, as if to erase all that related to the message. He didn't know what he felt anymore. There was a message from Susannah late last night, which he hadn't been able to answer yet. He needed to sort himself out and quickly.

Without further ado, he picked up his mobile and sent a text to Rob. It read: - *Didn't want to wake you. How about we meet in the Indian Haweli, 8 p.m.? G*

This was a very pleasant Indian restaurant on The Broadway in Barnes, so was convenient for both to meet there.

This was all he could cope with right now, just to arrange to talk. Beyond that he had no idea where next. Within seconds Rob replied with: - *See you there. X*

*

Kirstin and Susannah had returned to the Monte Carlo Bay Hotel after a sensational afternoon at the Oceanographic Museum. The Museum presents more than 6,000 specimens in their reconstructed natural habitat. They discovered some of the amazing species of the Mediterranean, the incredible diversity of the inhabitants of the coral reef and the monumental Shark Lagoon, all under the same roof.

They could not see it all but tried to incorporate the maximum they could in the time available. They finally made their way to the West Terrace, to the lounge at Turtle Island, for a well-deserved large gin and tonic.

The Museum's panoramic terrace was a magnificent setting, between the sea and the mountain. In addition to its 360-degree view over the Mediterranean and Monaco, the Sea Temple, as this environment was named, provided a unique chance to get up close to some African spurred turtles, ancient reptiles all now under threat of extinction. The whole experience was remarkable and one that Kirstin and Susannah would never forget.

It was now around 7 p.m., so the women decided to have a quick shower and change for dinner, which tonight they had decided would be in the Hotel's Le Blue Bay restaurant. It had been awarded a Michelin star in 2015, so was certainly worth a try. It had been such an exhausting afternoon that both Kirstin and Susannah hadn't the strength to venture out anywhere else this evening. They hoped they would have a chance to chat with some of the other guests they had met at the Casino, as several mentioned the excellent food and extensive menu at the Le Blue Bay.

Kirstin and Susannah entered Le Blue Bay restaurant just after 8.30 p.m. They both looked stunning. Kirstin wore a soft ivory all-in-one jumpsuit; sleeveless, cool and elegant. Susannah wore a very pale lemon mid-length dress, sleeveless and with a daringly low back. Both wore quite high-heeled sandals. Kirstin's were a nude colour and Susannah's were more of a deep tan shade. They each carried small clutch bags in matching shades to their sandals. Several guests in the restaurant looked up as they entered, as they conveyed an air of sophistication and glamour.

They were shown to a table which was over the far side of the restaurant and was in an ideal spot to observe most of the restaurant and, more importantly, who was in it. They wanted to speak with people this evening, if possible, to see if they could find out any more information about the Casino incident, in which Max Tarrant was involved, before they arrived.

The women looked through the menu and wine list and were just about to beckon the waiter over, when their eyes were taken to some waving hands. It was Gladys, Jack, Felicity and Ed, plus another couple they didn't know. They were just entering the restaurant. The women waved back, and Gladys and co. were led to their table. Kirstin was pleased to see them. It would now be easy to chat with them all after dinner in the bar.

The waiter arrived at Kirstin and Susannah's table to take their order. Susannah ordered Fried Ravioli, Stuffed with Seasonal Vegetables followed by Mediterranean Sea Bass, Kassava Semolina, Vegetables and Quinoa. Kirstin chose Contemporary Arancin, which was Artichoke and Shrimps, flavoured with Jamaican Pepper, followed by Mediterranean Sole Fish, Poached in Atoumaux Broth, Salsifies and Sweet Potato. They ordered a bottle of Pinot Grigio and a large bottle of sparkling water.

They relaxed back into their seats and gently shook out the pale pink serviettes and placed them on their laps. Kirstin quickly scanned the restaurant to see if there was anyone else she knew or recognised. At that moment, three men walked up to the entrance of the restaurant and peered in, as if looking for someone. The Head Waiter asked if they required a table. One of the men put his hand up, indicating not now but checked his watch and gave a time, which the Head Waiter recorded on his pad. The men left. Kirstin had already nudged Susannah, who also witnessed this exchange and realised they were the three men Kirstin had mentioned at breakfast the previous morning.

Both women glanced at each other but didn't comment as the wine waiter arrived at their table but each knew what the other was thinking. What were they up to? There was just something about them that transferred a feeling of caution.

They clinked their glasses and took a few sips of wine and were starting to feel much more relaxed after their hectic afternoon at the Oceanographic Museum. Susannah had placed her mobile on the table beside her, which was something she never did. Kirstin was curious and asked if she was expecting a call or message. Susannah knew she was overacting but she was concerned she hadn't had a reply to her text to Greg the other evening, well early morning. He was usually prompt at responding to her messages and she thought it was odd that there had been no response yet. Kirstin reassured her that it would be fine. He has probably gone to the pub with someone or was playing squash. Kirstin didn't want Susannah to worry but she was concerned for her. Kirstin had her suspicions about a few things concerning Greg, which she preferred to keep to herself now but hoped it wouldn't amount to anything of importance.

The waiter arrived with the starters, which were beautifully presented and resembled more of an artistic creation, rather than a plate of food. It seemed a shame to rearrange this exquisite masterpiece, but the power of hunger took over this thought very quickly.

The restaurant was extremely full and the noise level had risen considerably. Kirstin and Susannah had just about finished their meal and were looking forward to retiring to the bar, as it would probably be less busy, and they wouldn't have to raise their voices to hear each other.

The women moved from their seats and headed in the direction of the bar. Kirstin gave a quick wave to Gladys and her group of friends and indicated that they would see them in the bar later. Kirstin and Susannah found a quiet area of the bar to sit in and ordered another bottle of ice-cold Pinot Grigio. Susannah was still monitoring her phone but there was no message yet. Kirstin suggested she send another text, as maybe the first one never got there for some reason. These things happen sometimes. Susannah was reluctant to do that but decided she would if she hadn't had a message by tomorrow morning. At least that was a decision, so she put her mobile back in her clutch bag, out of sight.

It was not long before Gladys and her party arrived in the bar to join them. Gladys introduced the couple that Susannah and Kirstin didn't know as Olivia and Joe. Once they had got settled with their drinks, everyone started chatting about their day and on what trips and places of interest they had visited.

Kirstin made sure she was placed close to the new couple, Olivia and Joe, and Felicity and Ed, as there were things she wanted to ask. She had also found out that Olivia and Joe had been at the Casino too, on the same night as Gladys and Jack.

Olivia and Joe were from Vancouver, Canada, and seemed very pleasant people who were in their early fifties. They had been to Monaco many times over the years and always came back to this Hotel. They loved it. They had stayed in other Hotels in the location but rated the Monto Carlo Bay Hotel as supreme.

Kirstin turned her chair slightly so she was facing both Olivia and Joe and asked them about their horrific night at the Casino. Without a moment's hesitation, Joe, in his Canadian drawl, described that there had been an atmosphere that night, a feeling of tension. It was hard to express but whilst he was standing at a bar, he perceived security and staff were moving around the place with a greater sense of purpose. People in general appeared anxious and many observed the mood of security and staff, sensing something was wrong. Of course, there was something happening but exactly what was puzzling at the time.

Kirstin asked if they had witnessed any of the trouble directly or whether they had been in any danger. Olivia confirmed she was sat at a roulette table, where there was a man standing directly behind her, who was obviously in communication with someone via an earpiece, probably security. He was updating someone of another person's movements within the Casino. He was there for quite a while and then he ran to a staff entrance where someone handed him a gun. Olivia, now quite fearful, went to find Joe at that point. Joe concurred, they observed numerous armed security staff appear from different directions. This caused a massive disturbance and people fled, like antelopes being stalked by lions. It became very unnerving and then came the shooting. Chairs and many items were knocked over in the attempt to escape the gun fire. One man drew a handgun from a holster within his jacket. He fired several shots, but it was unclear who he was aiming at.

Olivia and Joe hid for a while behind some slot machines. The shooting was still going on so they didn't want to move. After a few minutes, the man with the hand-gun was stood nearby and caught sight of them behind the slot machines. He beckoned them to follow him towards a staff door. They crawled along the floor and through the entrance to safety. It was only a cupboard space, but they felt it was safer than being out in the Casino.

About an hour later, the place sounded quieter, so they peeked out of the door to see what was going on. It was mainly Casino staff milling around and police had now arrived too.

As they emerged from the small cupboard, the man who had assisted them came around the corner. He was bleeding from a gash to his head. He asked if they were all right and they thanked him for his assistance. His name was Max. They were very grateful to him.

Olivia and Joe continued to express their fear of that night but were still unsure what it was all about.

Felicity and Ed had also been listening to this episode of events in the Casino and confirmed the fear everyone felt. They too saw the man bleeding from a head wound. He was speaking to police when they arrived in very good French. He had only communicated to them in English and assumed he was English.

Kirstin remained silent, but thoughts were buzzing in her head.

Chapter 8

Phil Alexander-Browne was reversing his black BMW saloon into a parking space in Southend Hospital's car park. He'd received a call late on Sunday evening from his ex-wife Diane to say that his eldest son Tom, who was 30, was unfortunately in hospital due to a traffic accident. A lorry had apparently collided with his car on the A127 Arterial Road, as Tom was heading up to London. There had been an oil spillage of some sort and several accidents had occurred. Tom had suffered a few broken bones, including his leg and several gashes and bruises but nothing too serious.

However, Diane now lived in Scotland and couldn't come down to see him. Why not, Phil didn't know but he didn't ask anyway. Tom was currently living on his own, although he lived with his girlfriend

Lucy who was a teacher and living in London. Tom was working in Southend for a few months, as an ICT Consultant and Programmer but would then be back in London.

The hospital had said Tom was well enough to go home but that he would need someone to help him as he would not be able to manage on his own with no one at home. Diane had volunteered Phil and Kirstin to step in if they could and to have Tom stay with them meanwhile.

Of course, Phil didn't mind at all but wondered if Tom would prefer to go back to London to be with Lucy. He needed to judge the situation and assess how Tom was, before making any decisions.

Once inside the hospital, Phil was directed to Tom's ward. As far as Phil knew, Tom was not expecting him. Phil spotted him sitting in a chair, using his iPad. He greeted Tom with a hug around the shoulders, as there wasn't much else he could do with his leg in plaster and his arm in a sling. He looked battered and bruised around the head and face but otherwise in good spirits. Tom was thrilled to see his father, as it had been a few months since they had met up in London for a weekend. Phil went to collect a couple of coffees, so he could hear all about what had happened and what Tom wanted to do.

An hour or so later, Tom had reached the

conclusion that he would like to return to London but would need some assistance in getting there. He would have to terminate his time in Southend, as he was unfit for work and the company would have to organise someone else to do the job.

This was fine with Phil and he was thinking of the best way to arrange it all, when Tom's mobile rang. He took the call and Phil took himself off to find a bin for the coffee cups and a gents' toilet, to allow Tom some privacy with whoever was on the phone.

On his way back to the end of the ward, Phil wondered what on earth had happened, as he could see a nurse patting Tom's shoulder and seemingly expressing her sorrow. He could see as he got nearer that Tom was ashen and clearly upset. As Phil returned, the nurse moved away and indicated she would check on him later.

Tom asked Phil to sit down. He started to explain that he had not had a chance to tell any family member that Lucy was pregnant. They had both been delighted but as it was early days, they decided to wait to tell family. Unfortunately, that call was from Lucy's mum, who was with her in hospital, as she had suffered a miscarriage. They were keeping her in overnight and then she was going to stay with her parents for a while in Hampshire.

Phil was initially surprised but was extremely sorry

for them, if this was what they both wanted. Tom had been seeing Lucy for about two years and they had moved in together a few months ago.

This rather changed the goalposts as to what was to happen next. In view of this rather upsetting news Phil suggested that Tom come back with him to Harrogate, until Lucy knew when she would be back in London. Now, neither was in a fit state to help the other. Tom agreed and duly called the nurse over, whom he had been speaking to and told her he would be going to stay with his father for a while and would need all his belongings gathering up.

It was some time before they were on the road, travelling back to Harrogate. The journey would take several hours but they planned to stop off halfway to have a break and a drink. It was awkward for Tom to sit comfortably for too long, so it might be that they needed to stop a couple of times but there was no hurry. At least Tom had some company and support for a few days, particularly when he too was upset and sad that they had lost the baby.

Phil was thinking he must let Kirstin know the situation but was in no rush to worry her about anything at this point of her holiday. He would consider it later. She would be home in a few days anyway.

*

Kirstin was just waking up and was immediately thinking of the previous evening. It had been about 1 a.m. when they all retired to bed and she hadn't had a chance to speak to Susannah about any of the various conversations going on. She had arranged to meet Susannah as usual for breakfast at 10 a.m. She showered and dressed as quickly as she could, as she had overslept a little, it was 9.15 a.m. already.

Susannah was sitting sipping a coffee as Kirstin arrived. She didn't look her usual buoyant, lively self. She was always buzzing a bit in the mornings. Keen to chat and decide where they were going to go for the day, but Kirstin could see from her slouched posture and hangdog expression that something was clearly not right.

Kirstin indicated to the waiter that she would like some coffee and sat at the table. She cheerily said good morning to Susannah and took the coffee cup from the waiter. Susannah responded back but there was no brightness or lustre in her voice, as usually was the case. Kirstin didn't hold back and asked if she was okay this morning, as she seemed down. Susannah turned to her and, with concern in her eyes, clarified that she had still not heard from Greg. She had left it until today but was worried that there was still no word. Kirstin understood and felt the only way forward was to text him. Kirstin reiterated again that her original text may not have got there at all. She couldn't be sure but if it was worrying her, the best course of action was to send another. Susannah smiled and agreed she would after breakfast.

The women had cantaloupe melon, followed by scrambled eggs, with their usual accompaniments of grilled tomatoes and mushrooms plus more coffee. They had been looking through a guide book Kirstin had brought down and were deciding on places they might visit today. There were lots to see and do, it was difficult to choose. They finally opted to visit Monaco's most glamourous beach Larvotto, although man-made it is one of the most decadent stretches of sand in the world. They could sit on the beach and people watch, order a cocktail and relax. Then move onto an area full of character, La Condamine, where they could have the most diversified shopping experience ever, an estimated 200 shops scattered around the traditional market of Port Hercule. This might just be enough but if not, they could move on to Monaco Ville, the original town up on its rock, also known as Le Rocher.

The women left the table and arranged to meet back downstairs at reception in half an hour. Kirstin wanted to give Susannah some time to send a text to Greg, so she wouldn't fret any more about it, only of course if he didn't reply again. Kirstin decided they would cross that bridge when or if it happened. Hopefully not.

Susannah arrived at her room and sat down to tap in a text to Greg. It read: - *Don't know if you received my previous text but just wanted to know you were okay. Having a brilliant time here. Loving it! Let me know. S xx*

Susannah wanted to sound upbeat and not too concerned, so he wouldn't suspect her worry.

She felt better having sent the text. Deep down, she felt sure everything was fine, but it was slightly unusual for Greg not to have responded. She quickly gathered her things together for the day's outing and hurriedly made her way back down to reception. She had no sooner closed the door, when she walked directly into the path of two men, who were also in a hurry, almost running down the corridor. There immediately was a bit of scuffle, as neither could get past the other but in trying to do so, a small hand-gun propelled its way out of one of the men's inside pockets. Susannah was extremely alarmed and indicated this by gasping loudly. One of the men quickly retrieved it and held his hands up and appeared to apologise but Susannah couldn't understand what he had said. They disappeared within seconds and Susannah was left wondering if she had just imagined the whole incident, as it happened in just a flash. She stood for a few seconds before continuing down to reception. She felt a bit shaken and was pleased to see Kirstin was already there waiting for her. Kirstin could see something wasn't right and walked over to her immediately. She wondered if it was to do with Greg and the texting business but soon gathered it wasn't at all. Susannah moved away from the reception desk, so no one would hear what she was about to say. Kirstin waited with bated breath and could hardly imagine what she was about to hear.

Susannah explained what had happened and that she was sure the men were coming from the room where Kirstin had seen the man from breakfast the other day. Kirstin knew this was serious and something was very wrong but had no inkling as to exactly what it was all about at this moment. Susannah, who was still looking like a startled rabbit, wondered if they should inform reception of what had just occurred, but Kirstin was resolute this was to go no further.

The two women walked back towards reception and asked politely for a taxi to Larvotto beach. They proceeded to make their way to the entrance, where they would wait for their taxi to arrive in a few moments.

Susannah was slowly recovering and was beginning to feel more normal and calmer. She had never seen a real gun before and with the incident at the Casino last week, she was in her head linking the two events but without realising.

The taxi duly arrived within a couple of minutes and the women relaxed in the back with a sigh of relief that they were out of the hotel for a while. Susannah told Kirstin she had sent Greg another text and hoped to hear from him later. As if by magic, Susannah's mobile pinged and there on the screen was a message from Greg. Kirstin closed her eyes and thanked God. Better sooner rather than later for this to happen, otherwise she could forecast the day going downhill fast.

'Listen to what he's replied,' Susannah uttered, now positively upbeat from five minutes ago.

Sorry darling! Not good at looking after myself really. Rushing here and there. Busy at work too. Not as organised as you! Pleased you're having a lovely time. Speak soon.

G xx

Susannah was now smiling broadly and gave a little laugh when she read *'Not as organised as you!'* Thank goodness, pondered Kirstin. Now she could concentrate her mind on what was going on in their hotel and like Susannah, she too had connected this with the Casino shooting last week.

*

Greg stared at the message he had just sent to Susannah and felt disgusted with himself. He was yet to meet Rob this evening at the Haweli Indian restaurant and wasn't sure how he was going to handle the whole situation. He thought he loved Susannah but had not ever felt the need to marry, which he thought strange, as he assumed it was about desire and a bond-forming activity, so to speak. He wasn't sure about his own sexuality either. He liked the company and close companionship of men and was regularly out with them, even when Susannah was at home. He couldn't, for instance, see himself ever being without male companionship, as only being with Susannah wouldn't be enough. So, what was he saying, did he have feelings for Rob or was it just friendship? His mind was fluctuating around this subject for a while. He hoped it would become clearer once he had a chance to talk it through with Rob. Strangely enough, he was looking forward to the evening and felt consoled by the fact he could be frank and open with someone, who wouldn't judge him as odd.

He returned to his laptop to carry on with his work and temporarily lift his mood to a better place where he could slightly refocus and maintain his sanity.

Chapter 9

Phil and Tom finally reached Harrogate, after a very long drawn-out journey. They stopped at Services three times to enable Tom to have a stretch, as best he could, and to basically have a break from the monotony of the motorway.

They were now back at the house in Henshaw Gardens and whilst Phil gradually unloaded Tom's possessions and suitcase, Tom wandered into the kitchen and opened the fridge. One at a time he grabbed two beers and placed them on the oak table. It was now 7.30 p.m., and both were feeling exhausted. Phil came through to the kitchen and without hesitation prised off the tops of the beers and took an almighty swig, before leaning across the table to pass the other beer to Tom. Tom did exactly as Phil and both men observed that same wonderful feeling of sheer pleasure when ice-cold beer hits the back of your throat.

They decided the only option was to go and pick up a take-away of some sort, as cooking something was no longer viable due to the time. Phil loved cooking but after the journey and unloading, he'd had enough.

They went to the Indian restaurant, Shalimar in Cheltenham Parade, which was where Kirstin and Phil had been many times and found it quite good. Tom managed to hobble into the restaurant on his crutches, which was something he now needed to practise. He had taken off the sling, as his wrist was not too bad. They had another beer whilst they waited and were heading back home, all within an hour.

After their meal and a brief chat about arrangements for the morning and future arrangements for when Tom felt he wanted to return to London, they decided to turn in. They were both tired, after the day's twists and turns. Phil was working in the morning but said he would pop back around lunchtime to see how Tom was getting on.

As Phil was preparing for bed, he decided he would send Kirstin an e-mail tomorrow to let her know about Tom and of course Lucy. He imagined she would be a bit surprised but upset for them too.

Phil woke early at 5.30 a.m. and made the decision

to make some breakfast for Tom before he went into work. Once he was showered and dressed, he went down into the kitchen to prepare firstly some coffee, as this was an essential to be able to start the day, followed by some scrambled eggs and toast.

As a matter, of course, he switched on the TV to watch and listen to the Breakfast News. He was just about to put Tom's breakfast on a tray when there was a broadcast from a reporter in Monaco. Phil had not heard the beginning of this lead story, as he'd popped to the garage where their large American fridge/freezer stood boldly in the corner, as he needed more bread. The reporter stated that following the shooting last week in the Casino de Monte-Carlo, more information had come to light regarding who was responsible but at this moment police were unable to reveal any further details. What he did disclose was, SAS and Government Anti-Terrorist Agencies were involved. Phil was a little stunned by this information. He had heard something about it vaguely, a few days before Kirstin and Susannah went out there but hadn't fully taken it on board. Kirstin of course hadn't mentioned any of what she had since discovered, so all in all, this was a bit alarming for him.

As he was walking upstairs to take Tom his breakfast, he thought he would just mention it as an aside in his e-mail to Kirstin but obviously he didn't want to unease her in anyway.

Tom was extremely grateful for his breakfast in bed. He'd had a good night's sleep and felt a bit better, although he found it initially difficult to move much first thing in the morning, due to slight stiffness. Once he had sat up and had something to eat, he would attempt the next hurdle of getting out of bed and into the bathroom. Tom had an en-suite, so this wasn't so awkward but washing certainly was another major task, which took time. He had all the time in the world now, so this didn't matter.

Later that morning, Phil set about e-mailing Kirstin and explained how Tom was now staying with him, due to the accident. Also, that Lucy had lost the baby, which neither of them had known about or indeed anyone had known about. Consequently, Tom couldn't return to London as Lucy was staying in Hampshire with her parents until she felt fit. Phil thought it would all be sorted within a few days and that he would take Tom back to London by car.

He then asked if she'd heard any more information about the Casino shooting that had taken place just before they had left last week. He did not elaborate further and would wait to see what Kirstin replied. He hoped they were both having a good time and was looking forward to her arrival back home, when everything could return to normal.

At lunchtime around 2.00 p.m. Phil returned home, as promised, to check that Tom was okay. As he turned into the driveway, there was a silver VW Sirocco parked on the road but directly outside their house. He didn't think much of it, only that he hadn't seen it before. As he walked in, he could hear voices coming from the kitchen. He thought at first it was the TV or radio but quickly realised it was a voice he recognised. It was Diane, his first wife.

Diane was sat at the table with Tom and obviously had made him some lunch. It looked like beans on toast by the plates on the side. They were both having some tea and merrily chatting. Phil felt awkward and put out by this observation, as Tom hadn't mentioned Diane was coming down. He could have phoned him at the office just to let him know, surely.

Tom looked pleased to see Phil and very quickly conveyed that his mother had just turned up about an hour ago, unexpectedly. Diane went on to explain, as she could see Phil's steely look of not liking impromptu meetings of this kind. She had been speaking to George, their youngest son, on the phone last night and he had told her that Tom was staying with his father until he could go back to London. Also, he told her about Lucy. All this had been conveyed to George by Tom via text, on his way up in the car yesterday. Tom and George were very close, George being just two years younger than Tom. George lived in Edinburgh, not far from their mother. He was an architect and was doing very well for himself.

Consequently, when Diane knew all the information and that Kirstin was in Monaco, she decided to drive down early that morning to see how Tom was and to see what his plans were.

Phil felt extremely uncomfortable with Diane in his house, or rather in Kirstin's and his home. She had never set foot here before and Phil felt she had taken full advantage of Kirstin not being here and using it to snoop. Kirstin would be mortified, and she was likely to find out too. Anyway, there was nothing Phil could alter now, it had happened. He decided to leave them to it and excused himself by saying he had an appointment back at the office. If Tom was okay, he would remove himself from the situation.

Phil knew he could busy himself at work until at least 7.00 p.m., so he made it clear to Diane that she was welcome to stay until he returned from work. Without hesitation, she responded by saying she was driving back at around 6 p.m. and taking it easy up the A1. Phil was thankful, as it had crossed his mind that she may ask to stay, which he couldn't contemplate and would not have agreed to.

Breathing a sigh of relief, Phil returned to the office, pleased to be away from that uncomfortable encounter. He thought how ill-mannered it was that Diane hadn't had the decency to contact him to say this is what she was doing and hoped he didn't mind. He couldn't deny Tom a visit from his mother in the circumstances, but he would have preferred to have been alerted. It was all a bit of a shock to the system. On returning to the office, Phil poured himself a freshly-made strong black coffee and one of the secretaries popped out to grab him a sandwich, as he'd missed out on lunch too.

The rest of the afternoon passed quickly but Phil remained uneasy about the spontaneous arrival of his ex-wife. He knew she would be gone when he returned but he felt he needed a drink before making his way back to the house. This wasn't normally his style. He would be quite happy having a drink when he got home but for some reason, he wanted unfrequented solitude.

He left the office earlier than usual around 5.15 p.m. and drove around to find a parking space, somewhere near the Cuban Cocktail & Rum Bar Restaurant in Parliament Street. He and Kirstin had been there several times and had loved it. He felt like a cocktail, no rhyme or reason why but it was on his agenda now. He was madly trying to think of the cocktail they both had on their last visit, as it was amazing. He would recognise the name when he saw it, as his memory was out of gear and it was beginning to bug him.

He entered the cocktail bar and had a quick scan

around to see if there was anyone he knew. There were only a handful of people in there, as it was only 5.40 p.m. He didn't recognise anyone he knew, which pleased him, as he just wanted a peaceful drink. He checked out the list of cocktails as he sat down at the bar. The one he couldn't remember was at the top of the list, it was called 'Miami Vice' and was a mix of Bacardi Carta, Oro Rum, Coconut, Cream and Pineapple, mixed with Strawberry Daiquiri. *Wow, what a drink*, he mused and quickly caught the attention of the barman.

Phil sat back, he enjoyed watching the cocktails being prepared, it was all part of the fun. It took just a few minutes and *Voila*, there it was, spectacular and beautifully presented. A pale green straw hung over the side and loads of small ice balls bobbed about on the top. It was finished off with a slice of pineapple and a strawberry, which had been placed with precision, on the rim of the goblet. The stainless-steel goblet was ice cold on lifting and the first sip through the straw presented a magnificent feeling of true opulence and over-indulgence.

Phil was starting to feel more relaxed now but questioned why he had decided to come to the cocktail bar. It wasn't his usual haunt after work. He and Kirstin had frequented the place a few times, but it was usually on a Friday evening, after a busy week at work. Most evenings he was quite happy to have a beer or gin and tonic at home. Then it dawned on him; it was the not wanting to go home that was at the root of all this.

Phil's mind jumped back several years to before he got married to Diane. They had been seeing each for about two or three years before they got engaged and about a year later, married. Diane initially continued to work as a PA to the Executive Director of a large conglomerate. Two years down the line she became pregnant with Tom and after a further two years she was pregnant again with George, so she didn't return to work until both the boys were at school. Since then, she did many temping jobs and liked the variety and flexibility this gave her. Phil was trying to think where it all went wrong, as he thought they were happy enough and they had similar tastes and desires for the future but somewhere things altered dramatically.

Phil recalled Diane regularly going out with the girls from the office and obviously he looked after the boys while she did this, but it became a big part of her life. The girls were in constant touch with each other and had frequent girlie weekends. All in all, she became happier in their company. Eventually, this was what she wanted, so she settled down with another woman, whom she claimed she loved and couldn't imagine living without.

The shock for Phil was overwhelming at the time

and the two young boys were confused as to the new arrangement, sleeping at their mother's friend's house more regularly than they cared to do. They toed the line until eventually it all had to be explained. The boys adjusted and life carried on but there were wounds to heal.

Phil had felt let down by Diane. The boys were thrown into a situation that was difficult for them to understand and any form of normality wasn't reached for years. He looked back with sadness and a degree of contempt. How lives can be changed in the flick of a switch was uncanny. Did he have regrets? He did, as no one sets out on a path and wills it to fail. He wanted the best for his family, but this wasn't to be the case. He often wondered if Diane had any regrets. She seemed happy enough but who could tell. After reminiscing for a while longer, Phil thought he had better make tracks back home to see if Tom was okay. Diane would be gone by now, as it was 6.30 p.m.

Phil was in better spirits now. He had just needed time to himself to ponder. He was missing Kirstin, she kept him grounded and made him happy and content with life. They had a good relationship and were made for each other in every way. Meeting Kirstin was the best thing that had happened to him.

With a sigh of relief at it being the end of the day, he turned the corner in to Henshaw Gardens and decided he'd ask Tom if he fancied some fish and chips. He was sure he would and that would make tonight's meal an easy option.

Unfortunately for Phil, there in front of him was parked a silver VW Sirocco. Diane was still here. He turned into the drive and could feel his blood boiling. *What was she up to?* he wondered. Was she playing some sort of game? He couldn't imagine what she was going to say but whatever it was, she needed to leave.

Phil opened the front door and was struck by wafts of culinary odours, which immediately made his mouth water and heightened his senses.

Chapter 10

Susannah and Kirstin arrived at the small but very glamourous beach of Larvotto and decided to have a mooch around the area before settling on the beach.

The man-made beach was exceptionally clean, with clear waters. The whole area was extremely picturesque, with some stunning views. An excellent place to people and yacht watch, Susannah and Kirstin concluded.

They both noticed a handrail leading down to the sea and deciphered this was to allow those who were a little unsteady on their feet to access the sea. Kirstin had read that Monaco had the highest life expectancy in the world, so someone obviously had the foresight to erect this, allowing everyone to enjoy the water. Susannah had overheard a comment, whilst at the

Casino, that there was soon to be a multi-billion transformation of this area. Whether this would spoil its simplicity is another matter but both women were impressed with this place just as it was.

They decided to have a cocktail, as they were very close to what appeared to be a popular bar. It was busy, heaving with people but had an atmosphere of sophistication about it. Most people were sampling cocktails, in preference to other drinks, so it was a good decision. There were tables outside available, so they sat themselves down and waited for someone to come over to serve them. This truly was the life, and Kirstin was so pleased she had come here. It was a place she had always wanted to experience. She was going to recommend it for another time for her and Phil to visit. *I think he'll love it*, she thought. She wondered then how he was getting on and was missing his company considerably, particularly after all the goings on of the last couple of days.

At that very moment she heard her mobile jingle, indicating an e-mail arriving. She lent down to pick up her bag from by her foot and retrieved the mobile with curiosity.

It was from Phil, it read: -

Morning Darling! Just a few words to bring you up to speed with what has been happening in sunny Harrogate. I have Tom staying with me for a few days. He had an accident, where a lorry collided with his car on the A127 Arterial Road, due to an oil spillage. Tom has a few broken bones, including his leg and some bruises and gashes but nothing serious. Unfortunately, he is unable to manage on his own. He was going to return to London to be with Lucy, but we had an unexpected call from Lucy's mum to say she was in hospital having had a miscarriage. Lucy and Tom hadn't told anyone about the pregnancy at this early stage, so I was surprised to hear this but very sad for them both. Lucy is going to stay with her mother in Hampshire for a few days and will then return to London. When this happens, I will bring Tom back to their flat. Sorry to alarm you with all this but thought you ought to know.

Hope all is well with you both and that you're having a good time. As a matter of interest, have there been any more reports or information on the shooting at the Casino since you've been there? Heard nothing more here.

Speak soon. Take care.

Phil xx

Kirstin gasped when she read the e-mail, concerning Susannah, who was just ordering two special cocktails from the waiter and interrupted the flow of conversation. Kirstin re-read it again and passed her mobile across to Susannah for her to read it for herself. Susannah was obviously taken aback by the unfortunate news and hoped Kirstin wasn't too upset. After all, Tom wasn't her son and she had only met Lucy a couple of times. This aside, Kirstin was genuinely sorry and sad for poor Tom and the loss of their baby but what caught her attention more was Phil's final question. What did he mean exactly? Was he expecting there to be more news? Obviously, there was more news, but he hadn't been party to it, so what had triggered the question, she wondered?

After the shock of the news about Tom and Lucy, the women very much needed what was termed the 'Special Cocktail'. It was incredibly delicious, they both sat back and sipped their cocktails silently, each with their own thoughts. They people and boat watched for some time and found the overall atmosphere uplifting and exciting. It was a bit like life in the fast lane but having a snapshot of this sometimes stimulates the mind and brain.

They had nearly finished their cocktails and were deciding to move on in a few minutes, but first Kirstin needed to use the ladies' room inside the bar. She had to push past quite a few people to even reach the entrance. Once she was inside, she looked around for a sign indicating where the toilets were. Just as she had spotted it, her eyes suddenly fell on a face she thought she knew. Not instantly but then it suddenly clicked. The Casino. The waitress and the male customer. There they were, holding hands and looking romantically into each other's eyes. She quickly darted into the toilets, before either one of them looked up and noticed her staring.

Her heart was pounding. She wasn't sure why. It was just a man and woman having a drink and a chat. Yes, they were obviously an item but, so what. She had thought in the first place the waitress was giving him her number for a date arrangement. So why was she not fully convinced about this, of what appeared to be a platonic relationship? Why did she feel fearful? For some reason, she struggled to believe this was a normal relationship. She sensed scheming, planning something underhand but she had no idea what. As she was washing her hands, she decided she was being paranoid and would stop reading things into what in fact was an innocent situation. She would not mention this to Susannah, as she would be unsettled by it, particularly if Kirstin added her suspicions. No, she would just forget about the whole incident. She came out of the toilets and didn't even look across in that direction again, just in case they noticed her.

As she forged her way out of the exit again, she saw Susannah standing up looking out to sea in a complete world of her own. *What was she thinking?* Kirstin wondered. She was holding Kirstin's bag, ready for them to head towards La Condamine. They had opted not to sit on the beach, as originally planned, as time was whizzing by and they very much wanted some retail therapy time.

They observed a line of cabs further up the road,

so walked in their direction so they could be dropped off in the heart of La Condamine in a matter of a few minutes. Kirstin was still mulling over what she had just witnessed and was beginning to think the whole situation was nothing of concern and that she had jumped unrealistically to conclusions, irrationally surmising that something was untoward. Nonetheless, she was still going to stick to her view of keeping this to herself and not sharing what she had seen with Susannah.

Kirstin decided she would reply to Phil's e-mail when they returned to the Hotel and in the meantime, would think whether it was worth enlightening him with any details or events to date. She thought this probably wasn't such a good idea, as she didn't want to alarm or worry him unnecessarily.

La Condamine was bustling with people. It is an area found between Les Moneghetti and the Harbour of Monaco, right under the impressive sight of the Rock, on which the Prince's Palace rests. Susannah and Kirstin were not sure where to start but they had been informed through their guide book to go to Rue Grimaldi, Rue Millo and Rue Terrazzani, as these were filled with all sorts of specialists' shops. What that meant exactly the two women weren't sure, but it sounded expensive! Thereafter, they would visit the Princess Caroline pedestrian area where purchases, if any, could be made peacefully without the hindrance of cars, preventing wandering from one side of the street to the other, at random.

Kirstin couldn't get the incident out of her head. She was trying desperately to block it. Not wanting to be drawn into the recurring image in her head of the man and woman from the Casino. She couldn't concentrate, she felt hot, clammy and in turmoil. She wanted it all to go away. Her mind drifted to Phil's message and why he'd asked about any further details or information about the shooting. Where did that come from, unless he'd heard something else to trigger his mind. She knew him well and decided she'd hit the nail on the head with this deduction. She would look on the BBC News stories, as soon as she had an opportunity, without involving Susannah.

The women spent another hour or two wandering around the streets of La Condamine but were feeling quite weary, so decided to hail a taxi back to the Hotel. It seemed like they had walked miles. They needed something cool and refreshing. A gin and tonic came to mind, so they would head to the Blue Gin bar on arrival back at the Hotel.

They had made one or two small purchases, nothing too grand, to take back as gifts and momentoes but many places were expensive. They had a few days to go yet until the end of their break, so they thought they should not indulge too much at this stage. There was still plenty of time for more retail therapy later.

Once Kirstin and Susannah had arrived back at the hotel, they headed straight for the Blue Gin bar and were longing to sit and relax on the terrace with its beautiful views over the sea. They found a suitable spot and waved to a passing waiter, who immediately responded. Two large gin and tonics were on their way!

Both women relaxed back into their cushioned seats and were silent. They just consumed the opulent scenery, tranquil setting and pure luxury of the place. Within ten minutes, Kirstin noticed Susannah had fallen asleep. Trying not to wake her, she carefully removed the glass from her hand and placed it on a low table at her side.

This was an ideal opportunity to check the UK news on her mobile. Seconds later, she had a news update on the shooting in Monaco. It explained that further information had come to light, regarding who may be responsible for the attack. The police would not give any more details at this stage but did disclose that SAS and Government Anti-Terrorist Agencies were currently working with them.

Kirstin reread the article a couple of times before it truly sank in. So, there was something sinister going on after all. She sat and wondered, *what next?*

Chapter 11

Greg arrived at the Haweli Indian Restaurant on The Broadway in Barnes just before 8 p.m. Rob hadn't yet arrived, so Greg ordered a bottle of wine for the table and some mineral water. He decided to sit at the table rather than the bar, as it was private, and he wanted a few minutes' peace and quiet. His head had been a muddle all day and he was surprised at his own unsettled but excited feelings at this moment, as if he was meeting a first date. Immediately, he felt ashamed of feeling this way and tried to take a harder line with his thoughts and think about his family. What and how would they react to this mix of emotions and turmoil he was battling with? They would be disgusted, obviously, and would find the whole scenario a joke and totally unbelievable. They would disown him, have nothing more to do with him. Of course, that was only reasonable in the circumstances, and what about Susannah? Poor Susannah, how could he have treated her this way, after all these years. She had given him everything he ever wanted and was his soulmate in so many respects, but…

Why was there a 'but'? He didn't know. Why hadn't he been enthusiastic all those years ago to marry her like any normal person would have done? Perhaps that was it, he wasn't normal. Maybe he had always felt differently about his sexuality but hadn't recognised it or believed it to be anything out of the ordinary. He had always, since his school days, had many male pals, some closer than others and in later life he had acquired a very good social life with several male companions, whom he spent a lot of time with, usually playing or watching sport or going for a beer or two. He had thought this quite normal, but this relationship wasn't in the same category. This relationship held an emotional bond, a sensitive attachment, something quite different. He cared very much for Rob and this had become very apparent to him.

Greg took a large swig of the icy cold white wine and bit his lip hard with discernment and for a moment contemplated the outcome. Where was this heading?

At that moment, a head popped around the corner of his chair. It was Rob, smiling, cheerful and utterly relaxed. He squeezed Greg's shoulder tightly, as a show of affection and swung himself into the seat opposite. His face was lit up and Greg couldn't ever remember this chap looking so happy or buoyant. It was almost like he'd won the Lottery and was floating on air with gratitude to the universe. Happiness oozed from every pore, his whole body language was giving off a very different message. One that was starting to influence Greg's currently passive feelings.

The two men chatted flippantly about the day, whilst casting their eyes over the menu. A waiter approached the table to take their order. They had both decided. Greg ordered King Prawn Butterfly, followed by Lamb Tikka Biryani and Rob ordered Chicken Tikka starter and main course, Tandoori King Prawn. They added a couple of side dishes, Aloo Gobi and Tarka Dhal and a couple of plain and spicy Poppadums. The order complete, the waiter retreated.

Rob stared across at Greg, whilst he poured Rob a glass of wine. He needed to get sorted in his head, where he stood and whether Greg was reciprocal in his feelings towards him. He hardly dared to ask. It was unnerving but necessary to know where all this was leading, if anywhere.

Rob relaxed back into his seat and took a gulp of wine, hoping it would give him some Dutch courage to start this conversation. Without hesitation and quite out of the blue, Greg suddenly asked how he had felt about their Sunday evening together and whether he still held the same feelings now. Rob immediately admitted he did, even more so since he'd had time to reflect on it all. He had never felt so happy but wanted to make sure the feeling was mutual. Greg hesitated, as he couldn't answer. He had many more commitments than Rob, a family, grandchildren, and couldn't believe he was having this conversation. Something, however, was preventing him from saying this out loud and instead he retorted that he felt the same as Rob did. Something changed there and then; suddenly Rob and Greg were an item.

Although Greg could see this happening in full technicolor right in front of him, he was unable to put the brakes on, to stop it hurtling out of control. It was becoming more embedded by the minute and creating a situation that was to cause angst.

Rob put his hand gently on Greg's several times throughout the meal and it had a warm and comforting effect on Greg, to the point where he felt relaxed and secure in Rob's company. This was quite bizarre but somehow Greg was embroiling himself deeper and deeper into something that would alter his whole life forever.

After the meal, the two men finished off with a coffee and whisky liqueur, which allowed them time to decide where the rest of the evening was going. Greg had been toying with what to suggest and had at least thought of a constructive plan for now. Unfortunately, what he was about to say might not be exactly what Rob was hoping to hear but this had to go somewhere positively, at this moment in time, as there was no real way back. It had already gone too far.

Greg suggested that Rob move into Cleveland Road with him for a few days, so they could spend some quality time together. Greg needed to be sure this wasn't some sort of passing phase he was going through, or a type of mid-life crisis, although he was clearly over mid-life. Anyway, whatever it was or wasn't, he had to put some clarity to it and see how things mapped out.

Greg paid the bill, as he had intended, and the two men strolled back to Cleveland Road. Without any thought, they held hands at various points along the way. The only blessing was it was pitch-black and there was no one around to observe.

*

Back in the Blue Gin Bar, Kirstin was still preoccupied with the recent UK News she had been scrolling through on her mobile. Susannah had just stirred from her quick nap and looked around her quizzically, deciding where exactly she was and what she had missed, if anything. Kirstin assured her she had missed nothing at all and that having a quick nap was probably the best thing she could have done as

Kirstin was about to suggest an option which might incur a long evening ahead.

Kirstin waited a few minutes until Susannah had fully come around and had taken a swig of her now iceless gin and tonic.

'Do you fancy a night out this evening?' she asked Susannah tentatively.

'Yes, of course,' Susannah replied. 'Where do you have in mind?'

Without further ado. Kirstin suggested they use their complimentary vouchers to dine at Le Salon Rose at the Casino de Monte-Carlo. Monday would probably be a quiet evening to choose and they would be able to chat in peace and not be hassled by loads of people afterwards in the Casino. Susannah agreed this would be an excellent idea and a perfect end to a busy day. They decided to both have a long soak in their respective lavish baths and request reception to book them a table at Le Salon Rose at around 8.30 p.m.

With this organised, the women retreated to their rooms to relax in a sumptuous bath for a while and then spruce up for an exciting evening at the Casino.

Kirstin was still not going to mention to Susannah anything about the UK News update she had read earlier, as for one thing she didn't want to unnerve her and for another she wanted to try and unravel a few thoughts in her mind that were beginning to ring alarm bells.

Both women enjoyed the extra time they had provided themselves with for getting ready and felt thoroughly relaxed and refreshed after each having a bath, which they filled with a variety of expensive looking potions located on the surround of each bath.

What to wear was the next hurdle but once they were focused on the extent, or rather limited extent of their wardrobe, it was finally decided. Kirstin wore an all-in-one white soft cotton jumpsuit, with gold lace detail in the bodice. It was cool, lightweight and comfortable to wear. She added low-heeled gold shimmery shoes and matching across body bag. Simple but elegant. Susannah went for a pale pink, floral print, maxi dress, with three-quarter length sleeves. It was beautifully cut and accentuated Susannah's very desirable slim figure. She teamed this with the gold shoes and clutch bag she had purchased at the Metropole Shopping Centre and worn to the Casino on Saturday evening.

Within the next half an hour, they were both ready and had arranged to meet downstairs, at the Blue Gin Bar for 7.30 p.m. Their taxi was booked for 8.15 p.m., so they had time to relax with a drink first.

Susannah arrived first and chose a small table where Kirstin would easily spot her on entering the bar. There were a few people in the bar already, but it was reasonably quiet. Susannah thought she'd use the time until Kirstin arrived to send a text to Greg, to bring him up to speed with where they had visited and how he was occupying his time.

Greg heard and saw Susannah's text arrive on his phone, as they were finishing off in the Indian restaurant but decided to look and respond to this later. It was hardly the right time at this moment. He could see it was short, so wasn't concerned that anything was wrong.

Kirstin appeared at the entrance of the bar just as Susannah was putting her phone away. Kirstin realised that she must have sent Greg a message and hoped that he didn't wait too long to respond, like the last time, causing preventable anxiety to Susannah.

Susannah had already ordered the usual two large gin and tonics, which were heading to their table, as Kirstin was taking her seat. They both complimented each other on their appearance and clinked their glasses together for an exciting evening ahead. What that meant, neither of them knew but it was certainly a place of interest and intrigue.

The women chatted about where they might go tomorrow, maybe a bit further afield into Nice, for instance. However, they had several options and would decide finally over breakfast in the morning, depending on how they felt after tonight, as it was bound to be quite a late return home.

They finished their drinks and called at reception to drop off their room entry cards. The receptionist conveyed their taxi was waiting and Kirstin and Susannah walked towards the exit, where they could see the black Mercedes taxi waiting.

Just as they were about to push open the door leading to steps outside, four very smartly dressed Mediterranean men, who were talking non-stop, all at the same time, rudely hurried in front of them and climbed into the awaiting taxi. Susannah and Kirstin were speechless and couldn't believe what had just happened.

'Have they no manners!' screeched Kirstin.

She was outraged and turned on her heel to reception, where the staff had heard and seen the incident for themselves. They were extremely apologetic, but it was totally beyond their control. They ordered another taxi immediately and stated they would try and establish exactly who these men were and whether they were guests in the Hotel. They also would inform the taxi when it arrived that their fare would be paid for on the Hotel's account, as a gesture of goodwill.

The next taxi was only a matter of minutes, so there wasn't any problem, it was just the principle of it. Rude and arrogant men thinking they had a right to barge their way past and take someone's pre-booked taxi, showed no manners or concern for other people. Kirstin knew she needed to calm down, as this had rattled her cage. Susannah was much more forgiving and was no longer bothered. She just accepted it.

Chapter 12

Problems of a slightly different nature were unfolding in Henshaw Gardens, Harrogate. Phil walked through to the kitchen where he could hear all the activity taking place. Tom and Diane were sat at the table talking and peacefully having a glass of wine. Phil took a deep breath but before he could utter a word, Diane immediately apologised for still being there. She was organised and ready to leave at around 6 p.m. as she had said, and this was substantiated by Tom's frequently nodding head. She had said her goodbyes to Tom and off she went. Ten minutes later she was back, as her car wouldn't start. She tried to organise for the AA to come out, but it wasn't possible until the morning, so that was the reason and she hoped he didn't mind. Phil, short of saying he did mind and that she needed to find somewhere to stay, basically had to accept it. She was after all Tom's mother and he couldn't be seen to turn her out. This would not be fair to him.

Diane was half-way through cooking a shepherd's pie and had also made three prawn cocktails that were sitting in the fridge. She conveyed this was the least she could do in the circumstances. Phil remained silent and for a minute couldn't contemplate the thought of a whole evening in her company. However, that wasn't going to help anything, so he poured himself a glass of wine and sat at the table. He asked Tom how he was feeling and whether he'd heard anymore news from Lucy or her parents, which he hadn't. Diane got up to continue with the meal and Phil turned on the TV in the kitchen to try and mask the uneasiness and lack of conversation, which had dwindled. Tom was engrossed in the newspaper, so had turned his attention away from the awkwardness and was leaving it up to Phil and Diane to keep things civil.

The meal was finally ready around 8 p.m., by which time they had all had a couple of glasses of wine, which had assisted in a few pleasantries being muted, so it wasn't such a stilted atmosphere. Phil had set the table in the kitchen with mats and cutlery and the TV was featuring a good distraction for too much conversation.

They all sat around the table for their prawn cocktails, which were certainly tasty, and Phil was grateful to Tom for engaging his mother in conversation about all and sundry, which kept him out of it for most of the time.

The meal was very satisfying, and Phil thanked Diane for her efforts and for making it a healthier option to fish and chips. They remained in the kitchen until around 10 p.m. when Tom announced he was going to make a move up to bed, as the whole process would take him some time. Diane offered to help him, but he was adamant he could manage. Phil thought he had better show Diane to her room for the night. She duly followed him up the stairs. He provided her with towels and some bathroom toiletries he managed to randomly put together and left her to it. She seemed happy enough and said goodnight.

Phil returned downstairs to continue listening to the news and weather whilst clearing the final remnants of the meal into the dishwasher. He was feeling slightly uncomfortable about this whole scenario but what could he do but just accept it. Thank goodness Kirstin wasn't aware of it yet. She would be very put out by it all. Anyway, for the moment she didn't have to know.

Phil decided to turn in after the news, as he was quite tired with all the goings on and fuss of the day one way or another. He switched off all the lights downstairs and asked Tom if he was okay when he passed his room. There was no answer. Phil could see from there being no light under the door that he must be asleep, so left him. There was also no light showing under Diane's door, so thank goodness all this would be over tomorrow.

Phil entered his and Kirstin's room and turned on the small lamp by his side of the bed. He sat there a few moments, pondering the day and wishing that Kirstin was back. She would be in a few days and then they would celebrate her birthday. He walked into the en-suite bathroom, had a quick wash and cleaned his teeth. He thought he'd leave early and miss out on another encounter with Diane in the morning, if he could. He'd check on Tom and hopefully disappear to work before she appeared.

He returned from the bedroom, threw back the covers and climbed into bed. He turned off the lamp, rested his head gently on the pillow and closed his eyes. He must have drifted off almost immediately but was awakened suddenly. He felt extremely warm. He didn't wear PJ's for this reason, he was always warm. He sat up in bed and wondered if he'd left the heating on too high. He felt something touching his arm, he thought he had imagined it, but this was followed by someone saying they needed to get some sleep and an arm came around him.

Phil for a second could not comprehend what was going on but then his brain kicked into gear and he felt his blood boiling with anger and outrage. What was this woman doing? He leapt out of bed and grabbed his dressing gown that was hung over a chair. He screamed at Diane to get out of his room, which she did but very slowly and without reaction to his anger. She uttered not a single word and went back to her room. Phil's heart was beating faster and faster until he thought it would explode. He sat down on the end of the bed and tried to calm down by taking some deep breaths. He was beside himself with anger and he wanted to go and have this out with her. What did she think she was doing? She left him for another woman many years ago and was, as far as he knew, idyllically happy. What was her motive here? He would speak to her in the morning, when he would be calm, and ask her what she was playing at in no uncertain terms. Pulling a stunt like that was unbelievable. Phil was concerned he may have woken Tom when he shouted, so listened carefully for a few moments to see if he could hear anything. There was silence but that wasn't an indicator he hadn't heard but it would be evident in the morning if he had.

Phil got back into bed but was initially unable to sleep for quite some time. This had shaken him rigid. He finally dropped off but was no sooner woken by his alarm going off at 5.30 a.m. He was usually an early riser but this morning he felt exhausted and not ready to start the day at all. He immediately recalled the events of last night and again became angry and frustrated about what took place. *Diane needs to go but I must talk to her first.* He needed to know what had prompted that escapade and why?

After a shower, he quickly dressed and went down to empty the dishwasher. The house was silent, so he was grateful, allowing him some time to mull over and think what he was going to say. He decided to cook some breakfast for Tom and if Diane appeared, he'd do some for her, although reluctantly. Another half an hour passed, and Phil took up a breakfast tray for Tom. He knocked gently on the door and walked in. Tom was still asleep. It was 7 a.m. so Phil opened the curtains slightly to let in a small shaft of light. With that Tom stirred and turned over, spotting his father with the breakfast tray. He sat up and thanked him for making breakfast, yet again. Tom was enjoying being waited on but knew it couldn't go on for very much longer. He needed to make more effort in getting himself up and moving as soon as he could. Phil asked if he'd slept okay and Tom assured him he had, like a log, as he had been extremely tired last night. Tom queried if his mother was up yet and Phil responded coolly, with a 'don't know'.

On returning to the kitchen, Phil turned on the TV and started to eat his breakfast. Time was getting on and he was surprised he had heard no movement from upstairs. Perhaps she couldn't face him and was waiting until he had left for work. Fifteen more minutes passed, and Phil had finished his breakfast and was ready to leave. He decided to go upstairs and say bye to Tom and then knock on Diane's door. He couldn't just leave after last night's episode and say nothing. He climbed the stairs, with slight trepidation, and did not want to have a confrontation with Diane but something had to be said. He popped into Tom and said he would see him at lunchtime and make him lunch. With that he walked up a few stairs to the next floor, where Diane's room was situated. He took a deep breath and knocked gently on the door. There was no response. He tried again, this time slightly louder. No response. He put his hand on the round glass door knob and turned it to open. He tentatively pushed the door wider but could hear nor see anyone. The curtains were still shut, making it hard to see into the room properly. He called her name as he wondered if she was in the bathroom, but no one answered. He was now fully in the room and could see the bed had not been slept in. None of her belongings was there. Phil then caught sight of two envelopes on the chest of drawers. One had Tom's name on it and the other Phil's. He drew back the curtains and looked out of the window, which showed the road. Diane's silver VW Sirocco had gone.

Phil stood and stared for a moment and was gradually piecing the bits together, working out what was going on. *So*, he thought, *there was nothing wrong with the car after all, it was just an excuse to stay overnight.*

He took Tom the envelope and explained his mother had already left, which Tom found a little strange and queried about her car, which of course Phil could throw no light on but said they would talk about it at lunchtime and left for work in a hurry. Tom was bamboozled but accepted that they would talk later.

Phil shoved his envelope in his jacket pocket and shut the front door firmly behind him. He was in his office within 20 minutes and immediately organised some fresh black coffee. He turned on his laptop and whilst it was loading up, sat at his desk pondering. How was he going to explain this situation to Kirstin? It was beyond belief and sounded distinctly dodgy.

He sat sipping the hot coffee, adding just a smidgen of cold water to make it bearable to drink. He was not happy with the events that had taken place over the last couple of days, he felt uneasy and unsettled, wanting desperately to return to his normal existence with Kirstin and resume their normal life. He felt pathetic, as Kirstin would be home in a few days and all would be good again, so he needed to stop feeling hard done by and get on with the here and now.

He took a few more gulps of coffee and remembered the envelope in his inside jacket pocket. Should he just dispose of it? It was probably best not to know its content. The jacket hung on the back of his chair and as he turned sideways, he could see it jutting out of the pocket. It was a bit like a red rag to a bull. He wanted to grab it and rip it into fifty shreds. Diane had made him so angry, an emotion he rarely experienced nowadays. It was a betrayal of trickery and deception, all of which he found totally unnecessary and unfounded. Why had she stooped so low as to blatantly lie about her intentions or motive? If she had a problem, the honorable thing to do is to say so. Not that Phil would want to be involved but at least this would have been open and honest.

He made the decision to open the envelope. He gingerly took it out of his jacket pocket and cast his eyes at his name scrawled on the front. Diane never called him 'Phillip', always 'Phil', so that was unusual to start with and made it sound quite formal.

Just as he was about to open the envelope, his mobile rang. He could see it was Tom, as his name and number flashed up on the screen. He answered it quickly, as he wondered if he'd fallen or was unable to manage something. He was far from recovered, managing only small steps forward each day.

Phil only managed to say 'Hi', before Tom gushingly interrupted, with 'have you read the note?'

Phil responded by explaining he was just about to but what was the problem? There were a couple of seconds of silence from the other end of the phone.

'I'll let you read it for yourself, Dad,' came Tom's now sombre voice. 'It will be the same as mine.' The phone clicked off and Tom was gone.

Phil stared at the envelope that was lying on his desk. What was this going to reveal? He had a reluctance to open it at this moment, as already he felt a rush of adrenaline and he could feel a tenseness that affects anyone who is about to be told bad news.

Phil opened the envelope and pulled out a neatly folded letter, handwritten on pale blue paper, proper writing paper in fact, matching the envelope. This was not a rushed or scribbled note. This was a well-planned and thought out letter. It read: -

My Darling Phil,

My plans have not gone smoothly. They have angered and annoyed you. This was not the intention. In fact, it was far from my intention to cause either you, or Tom any grievance or harm. You are both very dear to me. Tom as my son and you as my ex-husband that I still deeply care for.

I wanted and needed to spend some quality time with you both, if I could. The opportunity arose unexpectedly through Tom coming to stay with you, so I took my chance to visit. You were no doubt angry and upset but I had no choice.

Phil, I have terminal cancer and have a matter of weeks to live. I'm not going into any details but there is no hope. I truly wanted to spend some 'Mum' time with Tom and some 'better memories' time with you. I guess I blew that by the bedroom scene. I suppose I needed a hug, nothing more. I made my bed many years ago when I left you and initially the boys, but I wanted to say thank you for the good years before this happened. They were good but I was ungrateful and had my own agenda, one which I now regret.

I've not gone about this in a very constructive way and should have been upfront from the start, probably then you would have had a little more respect for my unannounced arrival.

I am deeply sorry for any embarrassment this has caused you, but I hope in your heart you can forgive me and make amends with Kirstin over this mismanaged episode.

I know you will care for the boys.

All my love,

Diane. x

Phil found it difficult to take in what he had just read and for a few seconds, merely stared at the page. Obviously, he was totally unaware of Diane's illness and was unprepared for anything of this sort to come out of the blue in this way. Shock and sadness etched his face, his thoughts immediately turned to Tom and George, who both must be devastated after receiving this news.

He returned the letter to its envelope and slowly

placed it back in his inside jacket pocket. It was only 10.00 a.m. but he felt a gravitating need to return to Tom at home. He informed his PA he was finishing for the day, due to distressing family matters.

With that organised, Phil left the office and drove home to Henshaw Gardens, where he wasn't sure what to expect but at least he could be there for Tom. He would also contact George. They needed to talk.

On his arrival at 18, Henshaw Gardens he was unable to pull onto the driveway, as there was already a vehicle parked there. It was a police car.

Chapter 13

Kirstin and Susannah arrived at the Casino de Monte-Carlo dead-on 8.30 p.m. This was a little later than they expected due to the taxi incident back at the Hotel, involving four very ignorant men. Kirstin was past caring now, but it certainly had riled her at the time.

They decided to go straight up to Le Salon Rose, as they didn't want to arrive too late but also because they were both starving. They were ushered into the restaurant by the same very smartly dressed Restaurant Manager as before. They decided to ask for the same table as previously. It was available and was on the terrace but was quite secluded, well away from other tables.

The women settled themselves into their seats and ordered some wine, whilst they studied the usual extensive menu. A waiter quickly arrived with a large casket filled with ice, a bottle of Pinot Grigio and a bottle of sparkling water, both with their thin elegant necks poking out. How wonderful a bottle of wine could look presented in this way, making it all seem very special and luxurious, which of course it was. After all, this little trip was all about Kirstin's forthcoming 60th birthday, so this was a very pleasant warm-up to it.

The waiter poured the wine and sparkling water. The women clinked their glasses and were left to make their choices from the menu. This took some time, but they finally decided to share a Chateaubriand, with fresh vegetables of the day and to start, some fresh Langoustines cooked in garlic butter. A straightforward and simple choice tonight, nothing too complicated. Brain fog had started to set in, so they opted for simplicity.

The order was taken, and the women sat back in their seats, ready to enjoy the evening and pleased to have a second opportunity to dine at the Le Salon Rose, particularly as they weren't paying. Things couldn't be better.

Susannah asked if Kirstin had heard anymore from Phil, since his e-mail concerning Tom's accident. She hadn't of course but didn't want to mention his interest in the Casino shooting, so changed the subject quickly to Greg and asked if he was managing on his own. Susannah assumed so; his last text indicated he was fine, but she had sent him a brief message earlier.

Kirstin queried if they had made any plans for when Greg retired in a couple of years. Susannah smiled meekly and conveyed she hoped they would be married by that time and could devote more time to the family and grandchildren. Greg loved to spend time with the family, so she hoped he would do the honourable thing after all these years of being partners. It would make such a difference to how Susannah felt, if not particularly for Greg. Kirstin had felt sorry for Susannah over this stance with Greg over marriage but thought it would happen eventually.

Kirstin recalled a rather odd incident many years ago involving Greg and it had not entirely left her thoughts. They were all at a big party, a special occasion for someone. It was in London, at the Grosvenor House Hotel on Park Lane. For a minute, Kirstin couldn't remember who or what it was celebrating. Then it came to her. It was a chap called Ted Rogers. It was his 30th birthday party and he had just passed all his accountancy exams. He'd failed one or two along the way, so kept having to retake them, which took ages. He was working full-time and had a bit of a mad and very hectic social life, so achieving success at last was a delight and possibly a miracle. There must have been a couple of hundred people present at this celebration and most were staying in the hotel that night.

It finished, as expected, in the early hours and most people were worse for wear but Kirstin distinctly remembered getting out of the lift on whatever floor she was on and trying to find her room number, which was something like 246, but unfortunately, she had been trying to get into a room numbered 346 and hadn't realised she was on the wrong floor until someone opened the door. A man stood in front of her, totally naked. It was unfortunately Ted Rogers, whose party it was. It was not a pretty sight but to be truthful, he was oblivious and just shut the door again, not uttering a word. However, in the same room she did see, surprisingly enough, Greg Morton, sprawled on the bed, looking dazed and completely out of it. He didn't seem to be wearing much either, not a good situation to witness unexpectedly. She was unable to recall where Susannah was that night, but she had a feeling she was not present for some reason or another. This encounter, although many years ago, posed several questions for Kirstin, it kept cropping up in her mind. She had mentioned it to Phil, but he just shrugged his shoulders and conveyed it as just a silly night, where strange and random situations can occasionally happen. Kirstin totally disagreed with this assumption but let it drop, it was easier.

Their starters arrived and the women were then deep in conversation about a variety of topics and were unaware of anything else going on around them. They hadn't had many opportunities over the years to spend any length of time with each other. They didn't exactly live close by and both had their own work and life commitments, up until recently. Kirstin thought this was a bit sad really, as they had been friends for such a long time and could feel at ease in each other's company very quickly. They would automatically pick up from where they left off. The feeling was mutual, and it was comforting for them both to feel they had a true and reliable friendship, which would never disappear.

Since retiring, Kirstin had been thinking on and off about moving back to live somewhere on the outskirts of London. She felt Phil would probably like to do this too, when he eventually retired but that wouldn't be for a while, as he was only 55. They both liked London and many of the surrounding semi-rural areas. However, for the time being, she was quite happy with where she was, but it was a consideration for the future.

Their meal was nearly over. They were just finishing off the wine and were looking forward to going down into the Casino. It was approaching 11.00 p.m. It was a Monday evening, so they were not expecting alarming numbers of people to be there, but they did fancy a bit of a flutter and a cocktail.

They decided to play the slot machines first and would then order a cocktail to take to the roulette table. Kirstin was about to start playing when she noticed out the corner of her eye, that there were people she recognised sat over at a nearby roulette table. She stared for a moment, to gather her wits and question her eyesight, not wanting to be mistaken. She glanced around to pinpoint Susannah, who was engrossed in a game, on a machine further down. She was 99% certain that one of the men she was looking at was the same man from their Hotel, whose room was a few doors from Susannah's. There were a couple of other men with him, and although she assumed they were the men who were with him previously, she couldn't be entirely sure.

Suddenly, and without warning, there was an excruciating sound of an alarm. Everyone looked around in horror, as it was not entirely obvious what sort of alarm this was. Was it a fire alarm or a security alarm? Whatever it was, the few people who were in this area were looking around manically at which direction to go in. Within seconds, several staff appeared on the scene and were informing customers to leave the building immediately by the front entrance and to move well away from the building, once outside. Many people called cabs over to take them home or got into their cars and left as quickly as they could. Others were unsure what to do and stood around bemused as to what exactly was happening. Fortunately, it wasn't a busy evening and the number of people involved was considerably less than usual.

Susannah came rushing over to join Kirstin and both followed the guiding staff out to the car park. Once outside, Kirstin asked a member of staff what had happened. The reply was that an unexplained package had been found and that police were on their way. As he spoke, two police cars and a large police van arrived, sirens blaring, and several officers jumped out and ran into the Casino.

Susannah and Kirstin stood motionless for a moment, witnessing yet another couple of unmarked cars with flashing blue lights arrive. Six plain-clothed men exited these vehicles and headed inside, passing both women at speed. Kirstin gasped and put her hand to her mouth. Susannah looked at her alarmed face and asked what was wrong. Kirstin couldn't speak. She just froze to the spot. Colour drained from her face and Susannah could see she was now trembling.

'Did you see who that was, Susannah?' she mumbled, looking as though she was about to faint.

'No idea,' replied Susannah, who was extremely concerned about Kirstin's rapid decline and wondered if they should order a taxi immediately.

'That, Susannah, was Max Tarrant!' Kirstin conveyed with deliberation. The sound of horror and anguish could be heard in her voice.

Susannah was truly shocked by all this and made the immediate decision to call over one of the cabs that were queued up over the road. She waved frantically and was quite surprised of an instant acknowledgement. The cab pulled up a few feet from where they were standing. Susannah told the driver the name of their Hotel and they both climbed into the back. Kirstin remained silent and Susannah put a comforting arm around her. Neither woman spoke on their way back to the Hotel. Meanwhile, police cars with their sirens blaring continued to head towards the Casino, passing them on the road back to the Hotel.

On entering their Hotel, they went straight to the bar, where they ordered two large Glenmorangie's and two large black coffees. The best cure for shock they decided.

It was now after midnight and there were few people in the bar area, which was a relief as they just wanted to sit and not be disturbed. Kirstin was still in shock and was beginning to think she had imagined the whole thing and it had just been a bad dream. Susannah was being as comforting as she could, but she couldn't remember Max particularly, so couldn't corroborate that it was him. The effect on Kirstin was clear to see. She was devastated.

Seeing Max Tarrant in the flesh tonight wholeheartedly confirmed to Kirstin that he certainly wasn't a Game Show host in New York. No doubt this was some sort of cover up for what he was officially assigned to be doing. However, he may well have taken on the role as a Game Show host, on a few occasions, to cast authenticity over his employment. It was decidedly obvious to Kirstin that he was mixed up in some sort of government anti-terrorist activity, which was extremely concerning and dangerous. Not that she was concerned for his welfare but everyone else's.

Olivia and Joe, the couple from Vancouver, Canada, who were present at the Casino when there was the shooting with Gladys and Jack, had confirmed to Kirstin that a man called Max had assisted them at the Casino. He had a wound to his head and was carrying a handgun. Pieces of the jigsaw were starting to fit together and producing a scary picture. Physically seeing Max Tarrant had made the whole situation seem far worse, stirring up memories of the past and areas of Kirstin's life she would rather forget.

Kirstin and Susannah wondered what the outcome was of the evening's unidentified package situation and considered it could just have been that someone had left an item of their property behind, totally by accident. The Casino had high security systems in place and would have to act on this immediately, there was no question about it.

Kirstin was also curious why she hadn't spotted any of the men she had seen sitting at the roulette table, whom she thought were from the Hotel. She supposed they could have been guided through another exit and then left the premises, but it was odd. She didn't mention any of this to Susannah, as she was already shaky and uncomfortable about the whole scenario. Best keep it quiet for now, she decided. She had a feeling this was only the beginning of something much deeper and more sinister than she could anticipate.

It was now 2 a.m. and the women went up to their rooms. They arranged as usual to meet for breakfast at 10 a.m. What news would the morning bring?

Chapter 14

Phil parked his car on the road. He was curious and concerned of course as to why there was a police car parked on the drive and wondered whether he had accidently gone through a red light at some point during his travels from Southend-on-Sea up to Harrogate or whether it was regarding Tom's accident, where a lorry had collided with his car on the Arterial Road. Anyway, whatever it was, he had better find out.

He opened the front door and could hear voices coming from the sitting room. As he entered the room, a policewoman stood up, followed by her male colleague, who was holding a notebook and pen. They introduced themselves and asked if he would mind taking a seat. Phil glanced at Tom, who had his back to him as he had entered the room, now he could see him full on, as he took his seat. Tom was ashen, his eyes were red, and he had a look of total bewilderment on his face. He didn't utter a word nor did he look at his father. He held his head down, with his hands firmly clasped together.

The atmosphere was one of awkwardness and tension. Phil knew something bad was coming and he was unable to prevent it. He lent forward in his chair, as though to hint he was ready to hear whatever this might be. The next few minutes were to be the worst in his life, nothing of this magnitude had ever been bestowed on him. The Sergeant tightened his grip on his notebook as he turned directly to face Phil and proceeded to tell him there had been a very distressing accident, which had resulted in a fatality.

Immediately, Phil thought of Kirstin. Had something happened to her in Monaco? Before he could think beyond this point, the Sergeant went on to explain about a car journey, which led to a place called Burnmouth. Phil had never heard of such a place and was beginning to think whatever this was about was some sort of mistake.

Phil watched the Sergeant's mouth moving but he wasn't hearing him. Tom looked up and across at his father, realising the information wasn't penetrating, nor making any sense. The Sergeant asked whether Phil could confirm that Diane Edwards was his ex-wife.

Phil's mouth was dry, and he found he couldn't utter a word. The Sergeant asked his colleague to make Phil a strong cup of tea. Phil held his head in his hands, holding on to the few snippets of information he had taken in, which were whirling around in his head.

He looked up and asked if the Sergeant would mind repeating exactly what had happened, by this time the policewoman had returned with some tea. It was apparently the early hours of this morning that Diane had been driving back to Edinburgh. However, with only a short way to go, Diane turned off at a small fishing village called Burnmouth. It is located adjacent to the A1 road on the East coast of Scotland and is the first village in Scotland on the A1 after crossing the border with England. Diane drove through the village and out onto the coast road, where apparently for some time her vehicle was parked on the clifftop. This information was passed to police by a witness. Probably an hour later, her car was reported to have fallen on to rocks below the clifftop. The emergency services were immediately called and were on the scene very quickly. However, she was pronounced dead on their arrival.

Phil gulped his tea and felt tears well-up in his eyes as this awful tragedy sunk in. She was his ex-wife, but she was the mother of their sons and they had once had a very happy life together.

Phil asked the officers if they knew Diane had terminal cancer, which he and Tom had just found out about that morning. They confirmed Tom had explained this already. The Sergeant informed them there would obviously be a postmortem due to the circumstances, but that they would be back in touch again shortly, as there would be more information needed. For now, they wanted to leave Phil and Tom to have time together. They let themselves out.

For a few moments Phil and Tom sat in silence. Both trying to come to terms with what they had been told. It all seemed extremely unreal and so out of character for Diane to take her own life in this way. Her level of despair and depression must have been at rock bottom. Diane did have terminal cancer and she had split from her partner too, so she was on her own. Phil felt she had come down to see Tom, as this may have been her last opportunity. Being near to him for a while perhaps helped. If only she'd shared this information and hadn't gone down the bedroom scene fiasco, which with hindsight must have upset her. Tom wished his mother had told him sooner and certainly not in a letter. If he'd known, he would have gone to stay with her and perhaps they could have worked out something about her staying with him in London, so she wouldn't have been on her own. She could have had treatment in London, and she would have felt supported. This was a tragic end.

Phil and Tom suddenly both spoke at the same time, saying they must get in touch with George as soon as possible, and ask him to come over to stay, as he was on his own up in Edinburgh now and had only just been informed of his mother's death too, so needed to be with his family. Neither Phil nor Tom knew of any details about whether Diane had been having any treatment or if she'd been told how long she had to live, which made it all the more difficult to accept. There were so many unanswered questions. They were unaware of how long Diane had been split from her partner. Phil and Tom thought all this information would become evident when the police had the full facts of the incident.

Phil went to phone George and Tom made another cup of tea for them both. Initially, Phil could get no response from George, but he phoned back within a few minutes. In fact, the police had just left. He had been out on a job and no one could reach him. He was in a state of shock and not sure what to do or which way to turn. Phil immediately said he and Tom would come up for him and he was to stay with them until things could be sorted out. George was grateful. He just felt empty.

Phil and Tom had their tea and decided to leave by 12.00 midday, so they could be in Edinburgh in around 2 hours 45 minutes and hopefully be back early evening. Phil would drive, as Tom couldn't due to his injuries and Phil certainly wasn't expecting George to drive either. He was in shock. Phil's adrenaline was keeping him fired up and all he cared about was getting his two boys back to a safe place, where they could be together at this very sad time.

*

Kirstin woke early at 7 a.m. She didn't feel rested in the slightest, but her mind was still buzzing from the events of the evening before. She lay there thinking for a while what the outcome had been following the unidentified package that had been found. She decided to switch on the TV. The news luckily had just started, and she tentatively propped herself up against a couple of pillows so she had a comfortable position in which to view the full screen.

Within a few minutes the main headlines of the news rolled around, and initial highlights were given before beginning on more detailed reports. First up was the disruption to the Casino de Monte Carlo, by what was described as an unidentified package that had been found in the main part of the Casino. Very little was given away, as the report ended rather abruptly. The presenter stated that no other information was available, as the item found was being examined by experts, who were currently still carrying out their enquiries. *Another smoke screen*, Kirstin thought. With that, she decided to head in the shower and retreat downstairs for some strong black coffee. She guessed Susannah wouldn't be down too early, so she would have some thinking time to herself. She clicked off the TV, crawled out of bed and headed into the bathroom. She longed for the comfort of the warm water, the luxurious potions with which to anoint her body. The sophisticated fragrances, their major soothing qualities, which hopefully would restore her weary body into oblivion. She didn't relish the turmoil of the next few hours. There were too many questions without answers, adding Max Tarrant into the mix made it all too complex and disturbing.

Once dressed and ready, Kirstin made her way downstairs to the breakfast area. It was 9.30 a.m., so she had half an hour before Susannah was likely to appear. She found a quiet table away from where other people were sitting and asked a waiter for a pot of fresh coffee until her friend arrived, when they would order breakfast. The coffee arrived in a matter of minutes. Kirstin immediately poured herself a cup and decided to see if there was any more information about last night on her mobile. She clicked on the news items app and could see there was a picture of the Casino. The headline read 'Controlled Explosion of Package Carried Out at Casino'. With that, she read on but there was little explanation nor any real detail of what the package was or whom it might be connected to. It did, however, flirt with the suggestion it might be an act of terrorism.

This was becoming scary. Here in their midst was something developing on a larger scale than expected. Where was it leading, where would it end and more to the point, what next? Kirstin was wondering how much she would tell Susannah and of course Phil, as he would be sure to see the news and be concerned. She decided to put Susannah fully in the picture, as it was only fair now this had all happened. It would unsettle her, and no doubt put her off going to the Casino again, but often in situations of this type, you can't let circumstances stop you carrying on with life. She wouldn't rush to inform Phil. She would wait to see if he made contact first. There was no need to cause any disruption at this point. The overall incident was being played down. Nobody was getting too excited over it, nor wishing to give it massive air space, which was a wise decision.

Susannah arrived just before 10 a.m. She appeared a bit tired still and immediately grabbed a black coffee. She confirmed that she hadn't slept well after the disruption at the Casino. She just couldn't relax and kept going over the events of the evening. Including the sighting of Max Tarrant that Kirstin witnessed. Why on earth was he here?

They both ordered a full English breakfast, as they had a need for something substantial. Whether last night had given them an appetite or whether it was because it provided some sort of comfort, it was hard to decipher.

Kirstin brought Susannah up to speed with the various snippets of information she had come across, mainly by accident, but she confessed to Susannah that she had withheld these details from her as it could have amounted to absolutely nothing at all. If it was something of importance of course, she didn't want to create fear or anxiety, until she was sure of her facts.

Susannah perfectly understood and was grateful to Kirstin for her consideration but both realised now that there was something going on around them, which didn't seem quite right or add up particularly.

They both decided they wouldn't contact anyone at home about any of it and would just wait to see if they received any messages. They were unable to confirm anything anyway, except about the controlled explosion but even then, they had no other details. Best not to stir-up trouble where there currently wasn't any.

They decided to take another pot of fresh coffee out of the breakfast area with them and on to the terrace. They would sit and relax, watching the ocean and plan their day ahead. They had several places they wanted to visit, so they needed to make some decisions and not waste any more of their holiday on the if's and but's of what might or might not be going on. It would be purely guesswork anyway. A shot in the dark and all too serious to contemplate at this stage.

After an hour on the terrace and an empty pot of coffee, they made their way back to their individual rooms to freshen up and collect their belongings before heading out to St Nicholas Cathedral, the burial place of Princess Grace and other members of the Grimaldi family. Both women had read quite a bit about this burial ground and had been told Princess Grace's grave was part of the Monaco experience.

Chapter 15

Greg and Rob had spent a couple of evenings together now and life had suddenly taken on a strange role reversal of their commitments, sexuality and general interaction with each other. Greg had never considered he would ever be in a situation like this and there was a slight unease about it, which he couldn't shrug off entirely.

They obviously had not spent a weekend together yet, where they would spend 24/7 in each other's company, so at this point it seemed a bit of an unrealistic setting, where they just met up in the evenings for dinner and to spend the night.

Both men were warm and passionate to each other in every way. This didn't seem unnatural or taboo and Greg was surprised how he enjoyed the love and affection bestowed on him from another male. He'd never considered such a thought and although there was this slight wanting to push this feeling away, it wouldn't go. For the time being, he would see how it all progressed and evaluate it in a few days' time. A very methodical and constructive plan, but was he missing the point, deluding himself or just escaping from the realities of life?

He needed to get straight in his head how he felt about Susannah, his children and grandchildren. These circumstances do happen in life and he wouldn't be the first to claim he was the only person to find themselves in such an unprecedented situation, where one stood to lose everything and destroy a family unit.

Trawling this thought through his head made it all sound acceptable and a simple way of finding one's desire or fate. Did he have any way of deciphering or solving such a tragic dilemma? This truly was a dilemma and one he had certainly not envisaged hitting him at this stage of his life. No one, no matter what happened, or which way this eventually went, would be unscathed. It had already escalated beyond the point of no return, with dire consequences, if uncovered.

*

Phil and Tom were well on their way to Edinburgh to pick up George. Both were quiet with their own memories and thoughts, intertwining at a rapid rate, causing confusion, emotional upheaval and reaching a climax of disbelief. It was hard to understand and appreciate how each of them felt at this sad time, preventing the right words or phrases from being spoken. Each remained in the solitude of their thoughts, which was probably a therapeutic and healing process that needed to happen first, before coming to terms with the stark reality.

Phil wondered how George was coping on his own, having been without any family or close friends with him when the police called. He lived quite close to his mother and saw her on a regular basis. They would often meet up for lunch or go out for an evening meal. Phil wasn't sure of any circumstances relating to Diane's partner. He now knew they had split up but when that happened, he was unaware. It was strange he didn't know, as George was in regular contact with Tom and Tom would have mentioned it. However, it was irrelevant now.

They were coming to the turn off to Burnmouth and Phil dramatically said he was turning off. Tom stared at him but didn't utter a word. He found the coast road where Diane had driven to the cliff tops. It was strikingly beautiful and had a fresh, expansive feel, incorporating big skies and broad sprawling views that blow the mind clear of interruption.

From what he was told, Diane remained parked

for some time and he could sense her choosing to do this, as it was such a tranquil place of peace and beauty. He wondered if this was pre-planned or a moment of impulse, where she had reached a devastating low and could no longer carry on. If only she had come clean and explained her predicament. The boys were her family and although he was no longer her husband, he wouldn't have deserted her in her hour of need. She needed help and comfort, not to be alone, scared, afraid or regretting her life. The car was stationary, they both looked out to sea, tears replacing words.

*

Meanwhile, Kirstin and Susannah were ordering a taxi at reception to take them to St Nicholas Cathedral. They had heard so much about the Cathedral. It was certainly very grand and striking in appearance, from the illustrations in their travel guide.

Their taxi soon arrived, and the women were pleased to be setting out on a trip, as the antics of the evening before had truly jolted their self-confidence. Preferring to put all that behind them, they were out for a day of relaxation and cultural therapy.

Arriving at the Cathedral within what seemed like minutes, mainly due to their incessant chatting about the sighting of Max Tarrant and what appeared to be anti-terrorist officers, they clambered from the taxi and were immediately drawn to the beauty of this magnificent building.

The Roman-Byzantine-style building stood majestically in front of them. It was created in white stone, sourced from a place called La Turbie, Monaco. Leading up to the entrance, large palm trees soften the slightly stark architecture, but this didn't detract from its beauty and style. It was, of course, the burial ground of Princess Grace (Grace Kelly) in 1982 and later her husband Rainier lll in 2005.

The women stood for a while to glance around at the surrounding scenery and the amazing architecture. There was another building that took their attention, opposite the Cathedral, and Kirstin searched her bag for the travel guide so she could identify what it was exactly. She dragged the guide out of her bag and opened a map page, which gave the names of a variety buildings in the proximity. Within minutes she had established it was the Palais de Justice and informed Susannah that it was the location of Monaco's Supreme Court.

They wandered over to take a closer look before going into the Cathedral. Kirstin stepped into an opened door at the side of this building but was immediately met by a guard on duty, telling her she was not allowed in. Tourists are not allowed inside apparently but can admire the architecture of the building. Building commenced in 1924 and was completed in 1930. Kirstin referred to her guide book again and discovered the building was made of local sea stones that contained the remains of crustacean and mollusk shells, embedded in stone. She read on that a bust on one of the facades of the Palais de Justice is of Sovereign Honore ll. Sovereign Honore ll was responsible for ending Spanish rule and put Monaco under French control. Kirstin confirmed he was interred in St Nicholas Cathedral. They would look for his name once inside the Cathedral.

This was all fascinating information but didn't particularly resonate with either of them, so they decided to go back to the Cathedral. Susannah fancied a small bottle of water to take with her, so they did a slight detour to a small shop selling sandwiches, drinks and newspapers. Whilst Susannah was purchasing her water, Kirstin flipped over the pages of a newspaper on a stand nearby. The headline was about the controlled explosion, which had taken place at the Casino. It also commented on the enormous police presence, both uniformed and plain-clothed, and the involvement of the SAS. This all appeared very dramatic but suggested that there was clearly a lot more involved from what was being reported.

Susannah glanced over her shoulder and she too thought something more must be at the centre of this than purely an unidentified package. There was no mention of what this package contained and that was the mystery. Why were they keeping this quiet?

They turned to exit the shop when Kirstin suddenly grabbed hold of Susannah's shoulder and stopped her from opening the door. She pointed in the direction of the Palais de Justice. There were four men strolling around the outside and looking up and down at the building. They could merely be admiring the architecture, but Kirstin didn't think so, because she knew these were the four men from their Hotel, who were probably the four who had barged past them to commandeer their taxi.

The women watched within the 'safe-house' of the small shop, until the men disappeared around the other side of the building. Something was mighty suspicious here they reckoned. Visitors were encouraged to view this remarkable building from the outside, as they had been directed by the guard, but these men didn't fit the bill of the average tourist. They symbolised 'persons of interest', people to watch and keep a close eye on. There was something sinister in their behaviour and body language, suggesting they had a hidden agenda.

Kirstin and Susannah exited the shop and made their way back across the road to the Cathedral. They couldn't see the four men anywhere now and were somewhat relieved.

Inside the Cathedral it was cool, tranquil and

beautiful. There were many high arches, elaborate paintings of saints and the most stunning stained-glass windows, depicting aspects of history. The architecture was as impressive inside as outside, and the soft lighting and candles made a serene setting. The tombs of Princess Grace and Prince Rainier lll were plain and unassuming. Fresh flowers were purported to be laid every day. Kirstin and Susannah found it sad but moving that the Prince and Princess were both married and laid to rest in the Cathedral.

The women spent some time wandering around the Cathedral, which they found rich in culture, its awe-inspiring attention to detail, fascinating architecture, sculptures and wooden carvings. It was a sight to behold and one they truly would not have wanted to miss.

Strange as it may seem amongst all this splendor, there was a vending machine where you could buy a drink. Kirstin and Susannah decided a coffee would be a good idea. They could sit quietly in a pew, take in the sumptuous surroundings and relax. There were few people around at this moment, so the lack of movement and virtual silence provided a perfect time to reflect, meditate, be mindful, or whatever was required, to empty one's mind of distractions, concerns or irritations.

They were heading gingerly with their very full drinks towards a chosen pew, when they both dramatically stumbled to the ground with the impact of a thunderous loud bang, in fact several loud bangs. The two women stared at each other, mortified that they were now sitting on the floor of the Cathedral with their drinks spilt and possessions strewn all over the place. What on Earth had happened? They looked around but could see nothing which indicated any damage or problem. However, they could see a few people who had been inside the Cathedral, rushing outside at a rate of knots.

Kirstin and Susannah struggled to their feet, trembling and trying to gather their belongings as quickly as possible, as they were unsure what was happening. The loud bang or explosion or whatever it was, was certainly something major.

They rushed to the main exit and out into the open. They stopped in their tracks at the top of the many steps leading back down to the pavement. They could not believe their eyes. By this time, sirens could be heard and ambulances appeared from several side roads. There were suddenly armed police everywhere. People were scurrying all around, panic and fear had set in. The Palais de Justice had been bombed and stood in a state of ruin.

Chapter 16

After a few minutes, Phil got out of the car and walked slowly to the edge of the clifftop. He hesitantly glimpsed over and could see the jagged rocks below. There was not a chance anyone could have survived the steep drop or the impact on to the rocks below. A shiver went down his spine, his eyes welled with tears thinking of such a tragic loss of life.

Tom remained in the car and watched the stooping body of his father motionless on the edge of the cliff. It could have been so different, but it wasn't to be. With his mother leaving to move in with another woman, abandoning her family, there were no choices. It wasn't a great life for Tom and George when Diane decided she wanted the boys with her. They would have preferred to stay with Phil, but he had no control over the situation, and it was ordered by the judge that she would have custody. No one was prepared for this outcome or anything as extreme or sad. Tom wouldn't wish this feeling of helplessness on anyone. He felt in turmoil inside but was trying to stay strong for his father and of course George.

Phil returned to the car but was visibly shaken by visiting Diane's place of death. He apologised to Tom for veering off course so suddenly and for exposing Tom to the place where the tragedy had occurred. Tom reassured him it wasn't a problem and although he hadn't wanted to get out of the car, he was grateful he had seen where it had happened. The only consolation was that it was a very beautiful place.

They continued their journey back to the A1 and drove the final lap into Edinburgh. Tom sent George a quick text to let him know they were five minutes away. Phil didn't want to hang around and asked Tom to send George another text to that effect, so they could start their journey home immediately.

George had his front door open and a large case stood at his side ready. Phil greeted him by the car and gave him a big hug. Both shed a few tears but quickly regained their composure. Tom also got out of the car and organised George's case in the boot. He too embraced his brother, and both retreated into the back of the car. Tom thought it best to sit with George, so they could talk and let their father concentrate on their journey back to Harrogate.

Phil set off and could hear the boys talking, which was a positive sign and thought they would make each other feel better over the course of the journey. Phil wanted to get as far away as possible from Edinburgh and return to the comfort and security of home. He felt uprooted, anxious, depressed, saddened and unsure what was to come next. All he wanted was Kirstin. He felt lost without her, particularly in a situation like this, where he knew she would take charge and sort everything out. He needed to tell her at some point but today definitely wasn't the right time.

They arrived back in Harrogate at around 7 p.m. Tom helped George sort out his room and helped him unpack, whilst Phil went to collect some fish and chips. He also decided to pop in the nearest pub for a much-needed drink. The boys would benefit from being on their own for a while, so they could talk alone.

Phil ordered a large gin and tonic. He was thirsty and this was a good refreshing drink. He would collect the fish and chips afterwards and then they could all sit around the table and decide what needed to be organised.

Phil would also ask George about Diane's ex-partner, to see what happened there. Hopefully, the police would be calling again soon with an update and relevant procedures, so that would be helpful.

Phil decided he would go into work as usual

tomorrow but would be available if the police needed him. This would give the boys some space and Phil a clear head to think.

As he stood patiently in the queue waiting for their fish and chip supper, Phil wondered how and when would be best to contact Kirstin. He did need to explain everything to her, certainly before she got back. He had a nagging feeling about spoiling her break away. There was little she could do about anything anyway and it would only worry her. Tomorrow would be Wednesday, so he decided to see how the day panned out and try and come to some decision then.

Within the hour he was back at Henshaw Gardens. The boys were in the kitchen and had the presence of mind to turn on the oven to warm plates and set the table. Both seemed in better spirits and were chatting about football. Phil thought giving them some space together was what was needed. It was an incredibly awkward situation that had been bestowed on them all and some form of unity was now called for to be able to move on. Phil and the boys had always been close, so the joining of forces was never an issue and they would support each other for as long as it took.

It was now after 8 p.m. and all needed some sustenance, so were grateful for scrumptious fish and chips and mushy peas. Although this was a sad time, and one that none of them would ever forget because of the tragedy on the clifftop, it was a sort of reunion. A variety of unfortunate circumstances had somehow brought them back together as a family. Tom and the awful accident he had in Southend-on-Sea, followed by Lucy miscarrying their baby and now the tragic loss of Diane.

The three chatted until about 10.30 p.m. They discussed, along with many other issues, possible funeral arrangements, which was difficult, but they needed to think about it. Where this could be held? What sort of format would it take? Where her ashes might be scattered? Diane wanted to be cremated, she had mentioned this to the boys on several occasions over time but of course they would have to wait for the post-mortem and the release of the body, before any arrangements of this kind could be made.

Towards the end of their conversation, Phil finally broached the subject of Diane's partner. George confirmed her name was Lesley. Apparently, about a year ago they decided things weren't working out, more on Lesley's side than Diane's George thought, so they decided to split. The joint house was sold, and both went their separate ways. Diane didn't seem too bothered and soon bought herself a small property, which she loved, and seemed very happy. She joined a few clubs and just got on with life. Lesley moved away entirely, down South somewhere and with someone else, so that was the end of any communication.

Phil felt that all sounded very sad and was surprised that Diane didn't seem to be bothered. George added that she regularly went out, as she enjoyed walking and had joined a walking group and the gym and did play some golf with people she'd known previously. George just felt she had a lonely heart and that was the trouble when she found out she had cancer. She didn't tell anyone and took it all upon herself to deal with it. George's voice faltered, as he spoke about this and he couldn't understand why she'd kept this quiet; there were many people, including the three of them, that would have supported her. This is how she wanted it, although none of them was sure she meant to end her life as she did.

They decided to turn in, they were all tired and Phil was shattered with all the driving and emotional turmoil. Tomorrow was another day and maybe they would be able to set things in motion, if the police could confirm how long the Coroner required the body.

The boys went upstairs first. Phil generally cleared up and piled the debris of plates, cutlery and glasses into the dishwasher. He felt better for having had a chat with his sons, it had been a long time since they had all been together. He was going to talk to George about whether he wanted to move to Harrogate. Surely, he didn't want to stay in Edinburgh, although he did have a lot of friends there and had a very good social life too. It would have to be his decision and another conversation to be had when all had settled down. Tom was making good progress recovering from his injuries, so would certainly be wanting to return to London soon and reunite with Lucy. For now, though, all Phil wanted to do was to get some sleep.

*

Thick smoke billowed out of the Palais de Justice, two police helicopters hovered above and turned what seemed to be a brilliant cultural day into a mammoth moment of misery and mayhem. Kirstin and Susannah were unable to move down the steps which proudly fronted the Cathedral. They were mesmerised by the chaos, tragedy and evil that had been bestowed on this beautiful place. The architecture of the Palais de Justice was second to none. What a waste. What misery this would cause to the local people. There were stretchers and paramedics rushing in and out of the building, guided and rallied by many police, who were trying desperately not to lose control of the situation. Two fire-engines could be seen spraying vast amounts of water into the building, with little effect at present. Police cordoned off as much of the area as possible and it became evident that they wanted everyone out of the Cathedral and its surroundings, so Kirstin and

Susannah reluctantly, and still physically shaken, had to venture down the steps and walk to find somewhere to have a drink.

They were asked when they reached the bottom of the steps if they were all right, as a passing paramedic had noticed they were both diligently holding on to the side rail and taking it slowly on their descent to the pavement. They reassured him they were fine. Although it was only early afternoon, they both felt they needed an alcoholic drink, so looked around for a bar or something equivalent.

'This is becoming a holiday from hell,' Kirstin remarked, as she wobbled over the cobbled side street. Susannah agreed and wondered why there hadn't been a chance to lay or walk on a beach, where everything was relaxed and peaceful.

It was clear after this incident, and that of the previous evening at the Casino, that something very serious was going on. Most certainly terrorists were behind it, for whatever reason. Kirstin and Susannah felt they were in unsafe territory and this information would shortly be all over the world, meaning Phil and Greg would be extremely worried for their well-being.

They reached a bar, resembling a sort of shack but it sold alcohol, so it was fine. They asked immediately for two large Glenmorangie's with ice, which took the barman a bit by surprise. Kirstin thought he expected them to ask for tea or coffee, but that would not do at this moment in time.

The bar was very small and housed only four small tables. They sat as far away as they could from the actual bar, so they could have a bit of privacy. There were only two or three people in there, but voices needed to be kept down, as others could quite clearly hear every word.

They took several sips from their drinks and immediately started to feel the benefits of the alcohol warming their throats and chests. This was indeed comforting and allowed them both to relax a little, collecting their thoughts with a view to deciding on the next plan of action.

Suddenly, without warning the door of the small bar flung open, booted in fact, by a figure dressed in black and wearing a balaclava. He was brandishing a machine gun in the air and shouting something in a foreign language down the cobbled street. Everyone in the bar froze, there was silence. The figure stepped in followed by another, dressed the same. They grunted at the barman to pass them a bottle of brandy, which he did instantly. This was not a time to argue. Still nobody moved or uttered a word. A shot was fired into the ceiling and they were gone. Hearts could be heard beating and fear filled the air. What next? Where was this all going to end? Within a few minutes, people started to recover slightly from the ordeal and the barman called the police, although this was probably fruitless due to the emergency taking place down the road at the Palais de Justice.

The other people in the bar were talking about the incident and Kirstin and Susannah wondered if the two men were connected to the Palais de Justice. It seemed obvious they were, but they were not identifiable in any way.

They sat and finished their drinks and unfortunately were joined by the police, who arrived at the request of the barman. They had to give all their details and of course where they were staying. They would be contacting them within a day or two for statements.

Chapter 17

Greg's text response back to Susannah was short. It was only a matter of acknowledging and confirming that he was fine and coping without her, put in a caring way of course, and that he was delighted she was having such an enjoyable time. He sent it immediately, not wanting to focus too much on the content or the fact that he was living a lie.

This was a dangerous game, he knew that, but he needed to know how he felt and eradicate his dual feelings. How could he have lived all these years with Susannah, had children, grandchildren and not ever been tempted away by another man? If he was bisexual, surely, he would have had feelings or desires before now? He recalled there was someone in his life many years ago, he tried desperately to think of his name. He was temporarily attracted to this person for a while but thought it was probably more about being in a permanent drunken stupor at the time, than having any true feelings. The name came back to him, it was Ted Rogers. He wondered what had happened to him. He recalled it was Ted's 30th birthday party at the Grosvenor House Hotel, Park Lane, London. He couldn't remember much more, only he thought he was infatuated with him. He was divinely handsome.

Greg's thoughts drifted to his relationship with Rob and how he was looking forward to meeting him for a drink after work and then returning home for a quiet, intimate meal. He answered his own question about how come he hadn't had feelings before, well quite obviously, because he hadn't met the right one.

No matter what he felt right now, it was a massive dilemma affecting his current situation. Soon he would have to face the consequences of his actions. The realisation of blowing his whole world apart finally rang home and left a bitter-sweet taste. In a matter of days, life would take on a very different set of choices. Choices he didn't want to make but he couldn't have it both ways and this was causing him angst.

Greg had arranged to meet Rob in the Idle Hour Gastro Pub in the heart of Barnes, at 7 p.m. It was a stylish, cosy pub and Greg particularly enjoyed choosing from its twenty different varieties of gins and five different tonics. This being his favourite tipple, he was spoilt for choice.

Greg had a positive day at work and was feeling in good spirits and somewhat uplifted, probably because he was looking forward to meeting Rob. He had thought about their relationship several times that day, which was unusual. *What did that suggest?* he wondered. Was he becoming obsessed, pre-occupied with his new partner and lifestyle? He couldn't recall feeling this way after meeting Susannah. He and Susannah didn't usually meet in this way and of late, hadn't been out together so much. Was that an indication things were not as they should be? *Too many questions*, he told himself, *I'm analysing my predicament too much and it's not helping. I need to keep my mind neutral and uncomplicated for a while longer. My thoughts and feelings need a break,* he told himself sternly.

Greg was slightly late arriving at the Idle Hour, due to public transport issues. This time it was a hold up due to some poor person who'd decided to jump in front of a tube train. Taking their own life and leaving behind the people who cared, devastated. He could think of nothing worse. He understood feeling low, dejected and depressed were sometimes impossible emotions to overcome in today's world, but doesn't everyone have highs and lows? Maybe this person had mental health issues or was hooked on drugs, alcohol, who knows? There are many scenarios but none of them should be solved with the sacrifice of life.

Unfortunately, Greg had made a very good job of

depressing himself with these thoughts and so he decided to order a large gin and tonic whilst he waited for Rob. Rob would probably be held up too, as he would be on the same tube line.

His drink arrived and he grabbed a newspaper folded on a nearby stool. He'd have a quick glance through to pass the time. He turned a couple of pages and was met with a picture, albeit small, of Casino de Monte Carlo. The headline read 'Controlled Explosion of Package Carried Out at Casino'. Greg was taken aback. He hadn't heard any news that morning and he had been in meetings all day, so just hadn't touched base with any current news items. The article said very little and didn't elaborate on what the content of the package was or who they thought responsible. It could have just been someone's belongings. However, because it didn't say, probably meant it was more serious.

It was strange he hadn't had a text from Susannah about it. If it was serious, he knew she would have contacted him immediately. He would just send her a message and make sure all was okay. He grabbed his phone and tapped out a brief message. He didn't want to alarm her or Kirstin, if they didn't know, so he underplayed it.

Susannah darling, I've just read a short article in the paper about a controlled explosion of an unidentified package which was found at the Casino de Monte Carlo. It sounded straightforward and not particularly serious in anyway but wanted to check you were both okay.

Love G x

Greg pushed send and reverted to his gin and tonic and flipping the pages of the newspaper. He glanced at his watch and noticed it was now 7.30 p.m. He didn't particularly worry where Rob had got to, as he knew the problem. He would be here shortly and once they'd had a drink and a chat they would dine at home, where he had a homemade Shepherd's Pie from the freezer, waiting to be heated through. He had made this previously before Susannah had left, in preparation for his time alone. Although this bit wasn't quite the case, he would gladly share this with Rob, his Shepherd's Pies were something to behold, even if he said so himself.

Greg's phone pinged and there was a text back from Susannah. It read: -

Darling, everything is fine here. Much ado about nothing we think. We are safe, there is nothing untoward.

S xx

Greg gave a sigh of relief, *thank goodness for that*, he thought. It was now nearly 8.00 p.m. He would send Rob a text and tell him to go straight to the house, as time was marching on. They could have drinks whilst the Shepherd's Pie was heating through. Greg tapped this message into his phone and sent it. He downed the remaining drop of his gin and tonic, placed his glass on the counter and left.

Once home, Greg organised the table, drinks and put the Shepherd's Pie in the oven. He lit candles and dimmed the lights. Another hour passed and Greg was beginning to be concerned. Surely the holdup couldn't still be this bad. Something else must have happened. He didn't want to ring and pester Rob if he was stuck on a tube or waiting on a platform but in the end, he just couldn't leave it any longer.

He went to find his phone, which was on the kitchen table and was about to bring up the number keyboard, when he did a double-take of what he saw before him. There was the text he had just sent to Rob but the initials at the top of the text were SK and not RH. He had sent the text to Susannah, instead of Rob. He stood motionless and panic was starting to set in. Once a text is sent you can't retrieve it. Just like you can't put toothpaste back in the tube once squeezed. Horror and despair showed on his face. What was he going to do now? Could he explain away what he had sent? He couldn't think straight. Where was Rob? He would have to phone him; he couldn't mess about any longer. He needed his help.

Rob's phone was dead. Greg tried several times and assumed he'd not been able to charge it up or was in a poor signal area. He would wait a while longer and try again.

Meanwhile, he would sit and think what to do about the mis-sent text.

It was 10 p.m. No word from Rob. Suddenly, Greg's phone rang, and he was delighted to see Rob's name pop up on the screen. He grabbed it firmly and pushed accept.

'Hi, where are you?' he gasped down the phone, his breathing out of control. There wasn't an immediate response but then a voice said, 'Is that Greg Morton?'

Greg was unable to answer. He froze and just listened what was said to him. After a few minutes, he clicked off the phone and sat down on the nearest seat. Several minutes past before he could stand up to turn off the oven, blow out the candles and switch off the dimmed lights. He sat back down in the darkness and wept.

It was a police officer on the phone. They had accessed Greg's number from Rob's mobile. Rob had taken his own life on the tube track that night and the police had retrieved his bag which had been left on the platform. The police asked to speak to Greg tomorrow morning and would arrive around 9.00 a.m.

The night was a long one. Greg couldn't settle. He stayed slumped in the chair, not wanting to move. Braving it up to bed was out of the question. He couldn't stomach laying in the same bed he had slept in with Rob. The sweet scent of his body would be too much, let alone glimpsing at his toiletries neatly lined up on the bathroom shelf. It didn't bear thinking about.

Somehow, Greg must have dropped off, as he was awakened by a banging on the front door. He took a minute to come around and then realised who this would be. He heaved himself out of the chair and staggered to the front door, half dazed. He opened the door and let two police officers in, apologising for his unkempt appearance. He led them into the kitchen and invited them to take a seat at the table. He offered them coffee, as he was desperate for one himself. Once the trivialities were out of the way, the officers proceeded to enlighten Greg of the incident, which took place at Earls Court Tube Station.

It was horrendous to listen to, let alone imagine. They asked for next of kin. Rob had an ex-wife, no children, so Greg assumed it would be his parents, as he knew they lived in London. Greg explained Rob was a very close friend and had been staying with him for a while. He certainly didn't commit to anything else. He was questioned about Rob's state of mind and whether he had been suffering with any mental health issues. Greg explained Rob had in the past withdrawn from normality for a while when his marriage ended but that was some time ago. Lately, he seemed to have put this out of his mind and regularly saw friends and played sport. The officers were slightly baffled. They confirmed it wasn't an accident. They had several witness statements endorsing this but there didn't seem to be a motive. Obviously, there would be an autopsy, so something else might come to light, they would wait and see. The officers thanked Greg for his assistance and conveyed they would be back in touch, if any other information emerged.

Greg let the officers out and promptly walked upstairs, he desperately needed to have a shower and sort himself out. He would phone work to say he would be late, due to assisting police with an enquiry. He didn't need to elaborate at this point.

As he entered the bedroom he stopped in his tracks, as there on the neatly-made bed was an envelope. Greg stared at it, reluctant to pick it up. This was becoming the worst nightmare ever. He gingerly sat on the end of the bed and picked up the envelope. It had his name written on the front, in Rob's rather flamboyant handwriting. He studied it a while and thought how beautiful all the joins and flicks were, illustrating a very creative style. He opened it. It read: -

My Dearest Greg,

The last few days have been the happiest of my life. This perhaps sounds strange to you because you've not been able to see how happy my heart has felt. We have known each other for a long time. We have, over the years, become very good friends and this includes Susannah too. It has made me realise that I can no longer pursue our relationship, as it currently stands. It has reached a level for me of no return and in my heart of hearts, I know you are struggling with that thought or outcome. This relationship is never going to progress any further. I have been foolish to consider otherwise.

As an honourable man, you would not destroy your family unit to be with a potential loser. You and Susannah have been so good to me over the years, I cannot do this to either of you. I took a chance and made a very bad mistake but because you are a caring person you consoled me. This is probably more than a friendship, but I was wrong to lead you astray on my selfish merry dance.

I have never mentioned before but since my wife left me, I have been on anti-depressants and receiving regular counselling. What you see on the outside isn't what's going on inside. You weren't to know. I have many dark days. You made a massive difference to my self-esteem and self-confidence, but I can't let you carry on this façade, when I know your heart isn't fully with me and never will be.

I personally can't carry on, but I want to thank you with all my heart for the few idyllic days we have spent together. I will truly never forget your love, kindness, companionship, devotion and extraordinary compassion.

Forever yours,

Rob x

Chapter 18

Kirstin and Susannah stayed for a while longer in the bar after the police had left and basically tried to overcome their fear and anxiety that the last couple of events had created. Not many people will have been in a situation where one minute they are walking around a beautiful Cathedral, the next hearing an explosion which is the detonation of a nearby building, seeing horrific sights everywhere and finally being subjected to a man in a balaclava brandishing a machine gun, which he fired in the air to cause fear.

They followed their whiskies with a large black coffee each. The smell of fresh coffee and its strong and slightly bitter taste started to perk them up and bring about a more level-headed view of the situation. They decided they must shortly make their way back to the Hotel as a matter of urgency, as the horrific bomb blast of the Palais de Justice would be all over the news and they needed to contact Phil and Greg to let them know they were fine and not to worry. Also, they needed to inform the Hotel that the police would be calling at some point to take statements from them.

They left the bar and headed further up the road, where they could see some taxis parked up. They were feeling less shaky and more able to focus on getting themselves back to the Hotel and feeling safe. Once in the taxi they would be back within a very short space of time and then they would decide what to do first.

Walking through the doors of the Hotel was a relief and they immediately approached reception to let them know the circumstances of their day and explain that the police would be calling at some stage to talk through their events of what happened.

The Hotel were shocked, horrified and upset to hear of their plight and recommended they visit the Spa to have a luxurious massage, to help them relax and feel calm. The Manager of the Hotel was present whilst this conversation was going on and instantly conveyed it would be on the house if they cared to visit the Spa. The staff were extremely kind and considerate, and Kirstin and Susannah decided to accept the Spa offer. They would go to their rooms, change and meet at the Spa in half an hour.

On entering the Spa, there was a soft pungent smell of vanilla and patchouli. It was divine. The whole area was warm, welcoming, and immediately calming. They were ushered into a beautiful sweet-smelling room, lit only by candles. The couches were ready for them and two male masseurs awaited. Susannah did a double take of the very handsome men and turned to Kirstin, shrugging her shoulders and looking quite pleased. The women were left for a few moments to de-robe and settle on to the couches and arrange discreet coverage.

Both men returned within a few minutes and explained the procedure they were going to experience. It all sounded wonderful. It was going to take about an hour, then they would be left to relax for a while. Afterwards, a variety of fruit teas and other soothing cocktails would be available and served in another area of the Spa. They would be given soft white fluffy robes to snuggle into and could remain there until they were ready to leave. It was pure luxury and both women wondered how they were ever going to go back to a normal existence after all this. Little did they realise that their normal existences had completely changed.

The massage and pamper session was everything they could wish for. Both felt a million dollars. They felt revived, refreshed and vibrant after their experiences. It lifted their spirits beyond belief. They spent the whole afternoon at the Spa, or what was left of it after their morning's encounters, but it was precisely what they needed to recover.

They decided to eat at the Hotel restaurant that night and stay close to home, so to speak, as venturing out now seemed a liability and obviously, things were very raw after the casualties at the Palais de Justice. The women hadn't heard the details but would catch up with the news whilst getting ready for dinner later. They would also contact home and put everyone's minds at rest that they were safe.

The women were just replenishing their refreshments at the Spa when the receptionist popped her head around the door to inform them that there were two police officers to see them regarding their encounter this morning. This couldn't have been more aptly timed. Kirstin and Susannah carried their drinks into a side room where it was private. The officers didn't want any of the refreshments they were offered but preferred to move on with the job they had come for: asking questions and taking statements.

As the women may have seen slightly different aspects of what happened that morning, one officer would take Kirstin's account and the other Susannah's. They split into separate areas of the room, which had alcoves and comfortable seating. They were undisturbed and able to get through everything in about an hour and a half, which wasn't bad considering all the procedures that needed to be adhered to.

Finally, by early evening they were free of all constraints and able to relax on the terrace and admire the view. They both slumped into soft chairs and sighed, commenting on what a horrendous day it had been and one they would not forget in a hurry.

Suddenly, there was a clatter behind them. Both women shot around to see what was happening, their nerves not coping with being startled in this way. It was the girl from the Casino, whom Kirstin had seen handing something to a customer, and she assumed this was the customer she was with now. They were hand in hand but had obviously had too much to drink, as they had accidently tripped over a footstool and a chair, which had a domino effect on several other chairs that were close by. They were much the worse for wear, as they struggled to help each other up. The noise had aroused staff, several of them tried to assist in the righting of chairs and providing a steady hand. The couple were extremely embarrassed and tried to sidle out without further ado. As they were leaving, two men came over and started having a bit of an argument, prompting staff to move them off the terrace area and away. Kirstin recognised the two men as part of the group of four, who were sitting at the roulette table on the night of the suspect package. She was trying to put two and two together and recall whether they were also part of the four men that barged rudely past them, the other morning to take their taxi. She couldn't be sure. They were of Mediterranean origin and all looked a bit similar.

Kirstin looked at Susannah, who was trying to understand what was going on. Kirstin explained the connection, but it wasn't making any sense to her. Kirstin wondered why the woman from the Casino was here, she hadn't seen her here before, only in the pub when she went to the ladies, near Larvotto beach. There was something she was missing. She didn't like puzzles, and this was stretching her imagination to thoughts she would rather not be contemplating. She would keep her thoughts to herself. She knew she could easily jump to conclusions, so was reluctant to share any thoughts with Susannah at this stage.

After the kerfuffle with the drunken couple, they decided to retreat to their rooms to spend some time relaxing in a warm bath. They were still quite oily after their massage. They would also try and contact home and watch some news to see exactly what the damage had been at the Palais de Justice.

They called at reception on their way and thanked the staff and Manager for their Spa treat, which truly assisted in a speedy recovery from the morning's events. They had given their individual statements to the police, so they were satisfied with what they had contributed and hopefully helped in what was a diabolical sequence of events. They strolled up to their rooms and arranged to meet in the Blue Gin bar around 8 p.m. They were both quite exhausted, both physically and mentally. Whatever next?

Susannah poured a deep, warm-scented bath. She just wanted to lay back and relax, slap on one of the complimentary facial masks, presented in a small white wicker basket, to try and refresh her skin and lift her spirits. She was beginning to feel anxious and worried, regarding the speed and scale of events, all of which smacked of some sort of terrorism. She knew Kirstin had been playing things down, probably for her benefit but there was no denying something seemed to be brewing. Unfortunately, it seemed to be around them.

She stepped tentatively into the rather hot bath, now full to the top with bubbles galore. She carefully added some cold water, to make it bearable to step in, fortunately as there was a deep layer of bubbles there was no fear of the water coming over the top. She settled herself, put on the face mask, put her head gently back on a rather luxurious pink sponge pillow and closed her eyes. *Heaven,* she thought, relaxing her body.

As she lay there contemplating the evening ahead and wondering what she fancied to eat, she heard her mobile give a message-receiving ping. She couldn't be bothered to move and decided whoever it was could wait. She hadn't checked her phone all day and wasn't sure where it was, probably tucked into a pocket in her bag. She would investigate later. It can't be anything urgent, otherwise whoever it was would have phoned. With that thought in her head, she ignored the occasional ping and went back to thinking about the evening ahead and what she might wear.

Susannah remained soaking in the bath for about 30 minutes and then rinsed off her face mask, which had left her skin feeling silky smooth and revitalised. She allowed the water to drain away from the bath and prepared to use the overhead shower to wash her hair and sponge down her body, with some refreshing milky-coloured shower wash, which was made with oatmeal and meant to soothe and smooth the skin. Unfortunately, her hands and feet resembled a wrinkled prune, having spent far too long in the bath but she didn't care, her skin would go back to normal shortly. When she had finished, she wrapped an extra-large, pink, fluffy bath-towel around herself and stepped out of the bath with care on to another deep-piled bath mat and collected a small towel off the heated towel rail to dry her hair. She was enjoying the height of luxury at the Hotel and thought it would be a lovely place to return to with Greg in the future.

She turned on a small kettle that was perched on a tray with other accompaniments and made herself a cup of raspberry and rosehip tea. The huge bath towel was hung over the heated rail and Susannah put on a white toweling dressing gown, so she could sit and sip her tea and check the exasperating pinging on her phone.

She grabbed her bag and brought it over to the armchair, where she was going to sit and where she'd placed her tea already on a small side table. The tea was lovely, very fruity and just what she needed at this moment. She slid her hand into one of the side pockets within her bag and pulled out her phone. She noticed it needed charging. She pressed the text message key and could see the message was from Greg. She smiled to herself thinking he must be getting lonely.

It read: -

Darling,

Please meet me at the house, as it is getting so late. We can have a drink whilst the Shepherd's Pie is heating through. I am starting to get very worried about where you've got to. I know there has been a hold up this evening, due to an incident at Earls Court Station but surely it can't still be a problem. Please send a message, although I am wondering if your phone isn't charged. I'm desperate to see you.

Greg x

Susannah stared at her phone in total disbelief. She felt sick, distraught, empty and was shaken to the core. What was this all about? Well it was obvious what it was all about but who was he seeing? She couldn't come to terms with the sentiment of this message. She kept re-reading it, thinking she may have misread it. It said what it said. This message was not meant for her. As far as she knew, in all the years they had been together, he had never deceived her. *Who was this woman?* she wondered. *Probably someone he worked with, where else would he meet anyone?* Her mind was going around in circles. Then suddenly and without warning, the tears came flooding and she sobbed uncontrollably.

After about ten minutes, Susannah sat back in the armchair, wiped her tears away and tried to console herself with the remainder of the fruit tea, which was somewhat cold but did the trick to a certain extent. What should she do now? Reply, phone him or nothing at all? With her clear head on she decided on the latter. Rushing in with both feet was not a good move. She was truly devastated, there had been no motive to suspect anything, nothing suspicious, no excuses. It didn't add up. He was obviously aware he'd sent the text to her in error, so what was he going to do about it? She decided to do nothing at all, although of course, he would hear all the news today about the Palais de Justice. She was going to contact him, so he would know they were all right, but this had put a different perspective on that idea.

She thought for a moment and decided to go

ahead and send her message. She would disregard what had been sent to her and wait for a reaction. She picked up her phone and began tapping in her message.

It read: -

Hi,

No doubt you will have heard through the media today that there has been a bomb in Monaco, which has destroyed most of the Palais de Justice. We were close by. It was horrific but we are fine. It has been a scary day with men in balaclavas brandishing machine guns, but we are safe. The police have taken statements. We all need to be vigilant at this crucial time. There is no need for anyone to panic, so please reassure the children and grandchildren that we are safe and well. We are home in a few days.

S x

The last seven words stuck in her head. How was she going to return home? To what? To whom? Maybe, there would be no one to return home to. She felt unnaturally calm. She had got something off her chest. She had solved a difficult situation by facing it full on. She wasn't an overly confident person, but she had suddenly found an inner strength she hadn't realised she possessed.

Chapter 19

Phil was making breakfast at Henshaw Gardens. A cooked breakfast for all. He'd told Tom and George to be down for 10.00 a.m. He would be going into work later for a few hours but needed to be around for some of the day for the boys' sake and if the police returned.

Breakfast TV was on as usual, Phil was half listening whilst he set the table and emptied the dishwasher from last night's fish and chip supper. The news update was coming on and he could see a variety of film clips showing billowing smoke coming from a building, which looked in the state of collapse. There were police, ambulances, firemen and people with stretchers all around. The wording underneath read, *Bomb goes off at Palais de Justice, Monaco. Several seriously injured. Police believe this is an act of terrorism.* Phil re-read the words and continued to watch the pictures on the screen. This is the second incident of this nature, he recalled. The first being the controlled explosion carried out on an unidentified package, at the Casino de Monte Carlo. He grabbed the TV control and turned up the volume. The broadcaster repeated the information written below, adding that the SAS and the US Anti-Terrorist Agency were also assisting the French Police in their enquiries.

Phil concluded this was becoming more serious and was surprised he hadn't heard from Kirstin. He also wondered why the US Anti-Terrorist Agency were involved and could only surmise it was because it was of International concern. He was slightly panicked by this and thought, in the circumstances, he would have heard from Kirstin. He understood her motto was not to alarm people unnecessarily, but he needed to know she was safe. If he phoned her now, he would also have to explain what had happened to Diane. He could do this briefly, he supposed, he didn't have to elaborate or go into too much detail at this point. She would be home in a few days anyway. With that sorted in his head, he continued with the breakfast and could hear the boys coming downstairs.

Phil explained to Tom and George what he had just heard on the TV and, as the news came around again, they could watch it for themselves. They both agreed with Phil, he should phone Kirstin to make sure they were both safe and of course to break the awful news about Diane.

Phil decided he would phone Kirstin from the office where it would be more private. Once breakfast was over, he would leave. Tom and George had instructions to let him know if the police wanted to speak with him and that he would pop back.

*

Kirstin soaked for a while in a steamy, fragranced bath, before washing her hair and generally getting ready, albeit slowly, for the evening. She was still trying to piece everything together that had happened over the last few days, but nothing was making sense. She now believed this was to do with some terrorist organisation, but the real politics behind it deluded her. She was certain Max Tarrant was part of it all too but the connection between the girl in the Casino, the men in the Hotel with guns and the overzealous Ricardo Lucca, presenting complimentary tickets to dine at the Le Salon Rose, were all a very mixed combination of events.

She slumped into her armchair, snuggled in her toweling robe and then decided she needed a drink. She hadn't had anything out of the mini-bar in her room but whilst her mind was racing with thoughts, a gin and tonic would assist. She poured out her drink and tucked her feet under before sitting back into the armchair. She began again, going through the incidents that had taken place, the strangeness, the coincidences, the gradual intensity and now the destruction and injury. This started as nothing much but had clearly grown into something much bigger. It always was to be much bigger but to get bigger you must start small, if this makes sense. There was a plan, a well-organised plan and it was closer to home than she had anticipated. She predicted there was more to come. She was already on red alert. Her wits were heightened, and she could almost smell the trepidation approaching. She wondered if she was being over-dramatic but attempting to plant explosives, blowing buildings and people up, are not exactly mundane. Whoever these people are, they will stop at nothing, to achieve their goal. It was beginning to occur to her that they were on the edge of a rapidly intensifying situation, that was going to erupt like a volcano, given a chance.

She tried to calm herself down, as by her own scaremongering, she now felt fearful and concerned. Somehow, she and Susannah were involved. How could they be? That was a ridiculous thought, she dismissed it immediately. She certainly wasn't attempting to be a Miss Marple but even she would not be able to ignore the depths of secrecy going on. She felt it in the air.

There were people in her midst that were planning

and organising something big. It was connected to this Hotel, the Casino de Monte Carlo and Palais de Justice. She sat bolt upright in the armchair and looked straight ahead. How could she have been so stupid? All this was going on, under her nose. This Hotel was being used as the base; she was certain. The Mediterranean-looking men in the hotel, who were arguing, being aggressive, possessing a gun and barging people out of the way, were connected. They must be. She was sure they were also in the Casino the night of the package incident. One of them was probably escorting the girl in the Casino. She had seen them together holding hands in a bar near Larvotto beach. The girl in the Casino was a very useful connection. Was Ricardo Lucca involved? There was something strange about him too.

She needed to stop speculating, this was running away with her at an alarming rate. She would float it all past Susannah over dinner. She was much more down to earth and level-headed. With that sorted in her mind, Kirstin proceeded to select her clothes for the evening and dry her hair. She must also contact Phil, as a matter of urgency, before he heard any news reports.

It was nearly 8 p.m. and Kirstin was very nearly ready to wander down to the Blue Gin bar. She had calmed down considerably and felt silly she had wound herself up about everything. It wasn't typical of her. She could distance herself from things quite easily, but more was starting to evolve, and it wasn't a coincidence.

She decided to text Phil, as he surely would have seen or heard the news concerning the bombing of Palais de Justice and she didn't want him panicking. She rummaged in her bag for her mobile. She quickly tapped out a message. It read: -

Darling,

Please don't be alarmed about the news. I'm sure you'll have heard all about it by now. Sorry I didn't contact you sooner, but everything is fine here. We are safe and although this is a bit scary, we have no fears or worries. Hope all is well with you and Tom. We will be home in a couple of days, so loads to talk about then.

Please don't worry, take care.

Kirstin xx

Kirstin sent this immediately and hoped Phil would feel comforted that there were no problems. She didn't want to involve him in anything that was going on, it was too complicated and at a distance it always sounds much worse than it is.

With that matter dealt with, she scooped up her bag and left the room to go down to the Blue Gin bar. It was exactly 8 p.m. Susannah had not yet arrived, so Kirstin took the opportunity to order a gin and tonic and retain her calmness. Just as she was about to order, a man from reception approached her. She had spoken to him quite a few times and he was always friendly and helpful. She was taken by surprise at seeing him in the bar and wondered what on Earth he wanted. He politely asked if he could speak with her and directed her away from the bar. Kirstin felt slightly apprehensive.

He explained it was the police. They had sent one of their team to speak to her and Susannah about the incident in the bar near Palais de Justice. Kirstin was curious but conveyed it was no problem, although Susannah hadn't yet arrived. Kirstin glanced around to double check Susannah hadn't just turned up. She hadn't, but the man from the reception said it didn't matter, she could join them in a few minutes. He spoke to the waiter at the bar and indicated to let him know when Susannah arrived. The waiter nodded.

Kirstin was led around to the reception area and shown to a small private office situated behind the far end of the counter. The man from the reception opened the door and waved her in. The door closed and there sitting behind a desk was a man. A man she instantly recognised. The man was Max Tarrant.

Kirstin couldn't breathe, she couldn't move, she could only stare in total bewilderment. He seemed impassive, aloof even. Did he not recognise her, Kirstin wondered? Why didn't he say something?

There were a few moments of complete silence. Kirstin's heart was pounding, and she was trying to find the strength to speak. Before she could think of what to say, Max expressed how lovely it was to see her after all these years, but this was not a social call. He knew she was staying at the Hotel and had seen her and Susannah at the Casino. He explained he was Head of the US Anti-Terrorist Agency and was on undercover surveillance and interrogation duties. He knew she was aware of the recent incidents occurring in Monaco and denoted those responsible were part of an International Terrorist ring he had been tracking over several months. The US intelligence had indicated they expected more incidents of destruction and the SAS were in collaboration. The threat level was currently 'critical', and security was at its highest in Monaco. He wanted to check with her and Susannah what they had seen at the Palais de Justice and, as much detail as they could remember of the incident in the bar, involving the men with balaclavas.

Kirstin drew breath, about to react to his conversation but it was almost like talking to someone she had never met, let alone been married to for 10 years. He was expressionless, unmoved, insensitive, cold even in his reaction to seeing her and then proceeded to talk to her, as if she were some unknown witness.

Just as she was about to respond, there was a

gentle knock at the door. It was the man from reception popping his head around the door to say Susannah was here. Kirstin couldn't wait for her reaction. She may not remember him, but she was sure she might. Susannah walked in and observed Kirstin's startled rabbit look and glanced towards the desk. She froze for a moment but couldn't help herself blurt out 'Max Tarrant', to which he acknowledged, nodded his head and sarcastically retorted, 'correct'. Susannah's face was a picture of horror and anger. Kirstin indicated for her to sit down, before she either collapsed or punched him on the nose. She thought it quite amusing to observe people's different reactions to a familiar face, particularly a face of one who thinks so highly of himself. Susannah was now looking livid, due to his dismissive attitude about recognising him. He once again explained his reason for being at the Hotel and what information he needed to know from them, if any.

The women sat and went through their day explaining in detail exactly what took place from start to finish. In their view, there wasn't anything significant that stood out and they certainly couldn't identify anyone, due to the balaclavas. However, what they did raise were the incidents that had occurred in the Hotel regarding the group of four men, the handgun, the arguing, aggression and the girl from the Casino. Max was extremely interested in this and made notes. He would ask at reception which room the men were in and follow this through. It was a good lead. With that he stood up and muttered, something along the lines of no doubt he would be seeing them again soon, obviously thrilled to have seen them both again. As he headed to the door he stopped and turned, as if he'd forgotten something. He asked if they had enjoyed their complimentary meal at the Le Salon Rose. Kirstin and Susannah looked at each other, wondering how he knew but immediately said how lovely it had been but was a total surprise. To which Max replied, he was delighted they had enjoyed it. The door slammed behind him.

Chapter 20

Phil arrived at the office and poured a large cup of black coffee from a steaming filter jug. Freshly-filtered coffee was always on tap and he was particularly grateful for it this morning. The past few days had rather unsettled his normal pattern of living, bringing about tension and emotional trauma he hadn't anticipated. It was uncanny that these quite major events had all happened whilst Kirstin was away. If he needed anyone to keep him grounded, realistic and on an even keel, it was Kirstin. He wasn't good at being logical, level-headed or calm.

He was about to phone Kirstin and wanted to sound upbeat, as though there wasn't a care in the world, but he knew she would see through this veiled attempt of duplicity. As he took out his phone and finished putting in his pin number, a text message appeared on the screen from Kirstin. He hastily tried to read it, but it was quite long, so he switched to the text icon to see it in its entirety. He breathed a sigh of relief when he read it and was pleased everything was okay. However, this caused him a dilemma; should he still phone? He contemplated for a few minutes, taking large gulps of cooled black coffee at the same time. He decided it would be a mistake to phone her, considering the current home issues and if she and Susannah were safe, that's all he wanted to check. Instead, he replied to the text: -

Darling Kirstin,

So pleased to hear from you. I was just about to phone you but received your message. You say you are both safe and have not been involved in any of the awful problems. Thank goodness for that. Hearing the news was quite alarming. As you say you will be home in a couple of days, so try and enjoy the remaining time. Love to Susannah.

Take care.

Phil xx

No sooner had he sent the text than his mobile rang. He could see that it was Tom. What had happened now, he wondered. In fact, it was only to let him know that the police were coming around at 11 a.m. and would need to speak to him. Phil confirmed he'd be there and he'd see them later.

He sat back in his chair, deliberating how things

may pan out. If the police and Coroner agreed to release Diane's body, when would they have the funeral? The earliest would be Friday but Kirstin was due back on Friday. It would have to be Monday. It was going to be in Edinburgh they had decided, and the service conducted by an atheist. Diane never went to church and was a non-believer. She had no religious inclinations and would have approved of a humanist/freethinker service. Phil and the boys had muted the idea of her ashes being scattered on the beach a Burnmouth. She often went there to walk on the beach and loved the peace and tranquility of the place. She also loved the sea for its strength, power, total disregard, fluctuating into calmness, serene beauty and a soother of the soul.

At around 11 a.m. Phil arrived back at Henshaw Gardens. The police were already there and were sat having coffee with Tom and George. Phil joined them at the table and, as was expected, what followed was there were no suspicious circumstances regarding Diane's death. The verdict of death by suicide had been recorded, the body could be released. Phil needed to contact Diane's solicitor in Edinburgh, where the Will would be read. Phil assumed Diane's property, home contents, personnel possessions and money would be divided between Tom and George. Although this was an awful situation for Tom and George to find themselves in, it would enable them to get on the property ladder and give them some form of security for the future.

With this said, the police left and the three men fell silent at the thought of all the arrangements needing to be made over the next few days. Tom and George thought they should both go back to Edinburgh and sort as much as they could before planning the funeral. Phil thought this an excellent idea, as he didn't want to be involved in Diane's property or possessions etc. Best to let the boys sort it out between them. Phil would phone Diane's solicitor and arrange an appointment for the boys, as soon as possible.

George suggested he and Tom go back to Edinburgh on the train tomorrow, so they could get on with the arrangements and give Phil some time before Kirstin returned home. Phil was grateful, as he didn't want to be driving back and forth to Edinburgh. The boys would be better on their own sorting everything out, how they wanted it.

Tom needed to have the plaster cast removed from his leg. He had an appointment at the hospital later that afternoon, so was hoping this would be the case and he would be all right travelling tomorrow. George was going with him in a taxi and once back at home they would organise a train for late morning, if possible.

Phil started to feel much better, as though they

had turned a massive corner in this very sad situation. He suggested he rustle up some toasted sandwiches, salad and beers for lunch and then leave them to it and go back to work for the afternoon.

He was pleased he hadn't needed to phone Kirstin. Having a couple of days to gather his thoughts, tidy the house and put things back in the order they were, before Kirstin left, would be a brilliant opportunity. He was also pleased for his sons; in that they would benefit financially from their mother's estate, giving them a good start in life. That would have been all Diane would have wanted.

The three of them had a good lunch and chatted endlessly. The boys seemed in a better place and their spirits had been lifted by the news they could proceed with their mother's funeral arrangements. They now wanted to move on with their lives. Phil returned to the office feeling relieved and finally at ease.

*

Greg knew he had to show the police Rob's letter. It provided the reasoning behind Rob's actions and the evidence they would require; it was not an accident but suicide. The very thought made Greg wince. He had no option and he needed to get on with it. He would have a shower, go into work and later contact the police and explain he'd found a letter that might be of interest to them. Greg couldn't withhold evidence and although he didn't want anyone to know about Rob and his relationship, he had to face up to it.

He quickly showered and dressed for work. Downstairs in the kitchen, whilst grabbing a coffee and some toast, he re-read the letter. It was so poignant. It took his breath away. His eyes filled with tears; he couldn't comprehend Rob's actions. If only he'd talked about it with him. They could have been open, honest and thought through it together, wherever it was to lead. Now there was nothing. Greg felt despair, anger, fragility and hurt. He needed to leave the house and go into work; being home was unbearable.

He gathered his belongings, folded the letter, placing it back into its envelope and slid it into his pocket. He set off to catch a train into London and hopefully try to come to terms with what had happened. He blamed himself for Rob's actions, there was no doubt about that. He had responded to his advances and encouraged the relationship, instead of pushing it away. He had felt so much for him. He was attracted to him. He had great affection for Rob. He considered it to be love. Why was he trying to deny any of his true feelings?

The train journey to London was unpleasant, he couldn't focus, concentrate or think straight. How was he going to work? Suddenly, glancing out of the window he saw a billboard advertising the Monaco

Grand Prix, taking place on 28th May. It was advertising various luxury packages. Greg was brought back to his senses with a jolt. *Susannah, Susannah,* rang in his head. What was he going to do about Susannah? He instantly remembered about the text. He had sent Susannah the text meant for Rob. How was he going to explain? She would think it was another woman. That was probably worse than it being male. He couldn't imagine what she was thinking but he knew he had to do something before his entire life was totally messed up.

He had a little further to go before arriving at Piccadilly Station. He delved into his bag to locate his phone. He grabbed it, fumbling chaotically with the password entry, only to discover it was dead. He hadn't charged his phone. He hadn't brought his charger either but thought he had a spare at work. He could feel the heat of his body rising, his heart pounding, as though he was going to explode. He must calm himself; this wasn't doing him any good in the situation he now found himself.

He took some deep breaths, trying not to be too obvious about it, sitting in a carriage full of people. The woman next to him glanced up and he wondered if she thought he was about to have a heart attack. She might be right he supposed. He certainly was in a terrible state and all brought on by his own conduct. He was flattered by Rob, made to feel attractive, inspiring, worthy and confident. He wasn't particularly confident, strangely enough, even though he had to show he was in the work place but underneath, no he wasn't. Rob had brought all his attributes out. Made him feel he was somebody. Not just an anybody. Was this where he and Susannah had gone wrong? Did she make him feel inadequate? He couldn't think how she made him feel. Ordinary, came to mind. Just ordinary and probably boring too. He supposed Rob had made him feel valued. Valued is a very underestimated word, he considered it for a moment. It meant, respected, cherished, treasured and appreciated. Wholeheartedly, this is what Rob gave to him, the feeling of being valued.

The train ground to a halt and everyone was rushing in different directions, making their way here and there with their busy lives ahead of them. Greg couldn't move. He sat until he was all alone. There was no one left on the train. There was probably no one left in his life.

It took several minutes for him to be able to move. A guard walked past on the platform and then bobbed his head into the carriage, where Greg lamely sat, trying to recover his composure. He asked if he was okay. Greg was quick to respond, telling him he had fallen asleep and just woken. With that, he edged his way to the end of the seat and stood up, ready to exit the train.

He couldn't remember travelling the next part of his journey to South Kensington, but he had done it so many times, it was like clockwork. His thoughts were elsewhere and until he arrived at the office in Northcliffe House and was seated at his desk, he wasn't focused.

The first thing he needed to do was find the spare charger for his mobile. This was essential in enabling him to establish if anything had transpired from his mis-sent text to Susannah. Eventually, he found it, right at the back of a long deep drawer. He grappled with removing it from its hidden place, yanking it out with gusto and immediately reconciled it with his phone. It was quite dead, but it shouldn't take very long for it to restore some juice and be functional again. Whilst this mini-task was put into operation, Greg went to grab himself a much-deserved coffee, strong black coffee.

On his return, he quickly picked up his phone and observed its charging progress. Already it was 10%, enough to turn on and see what was there. There were several of the usual advertising e-mails and texts, but his eyes fell on the text with the initials SK at the top. Susannah Kingsley. Not SM, as it should be. He should have married her. What a fool he'd been all these years. Too late now. He clicked it open, revealing quite a long message. He scanned it quickly first looking for clues to its content. Harsh words, fury, anger, anything that suggested an acknowledgement of receiving that fateful text.

There was nothing. He re-read every word slowly and deliberately. This was an ordinary text. Well, it wasn't ordinary, as it spoke of the traumatic events relating to the bombing of the Palais de Justice and men brandishing machine guns, but as always, Susannah had thought of others being worried and not wanting anyone to panic. She wanted to spare those closest to her, including him from speculation and concern. She had put everyone's mind at peace. If only he could put her mind at peace.

He was convinced she had received the text meant for Rob, but she was showing resilience and strength in kicking it aside. Knowing deep down, somehow, they'd work it out. They would, he was certain.

Chapter 21

Kirstin and Susannah were left shell-shocked by the delightful Mr Max Tarrant. They had to float back down to reality from being propelled to the ceiling by this interjectory moment. Kirstin was overawed by this man's ruthless detachment and self-opinionated rapport with himself. How did she ever hero-worship this devil in disguise? Let alone marry him and be his wife for 10 years, or rather his doormat. She was reeling inside from his pompous self-righteous image and the total disrespect for their past relationship. She supposed it confirmed what she had known but never acknowledged all along, that he cared only for himself.

She reflected, and for a few minutes considered whether this was true or was it that her heart was truly bitter and twisted. She recalled the long letters home, when he was away in Singapore on various projects early in their lives. They were refreshing with loads of interesting news about where he was working and what he had seen but they were also caring, charming in fact, and showed a sort of tenderness, not self-centredness or arrogance. He wrote poetry for her and it was clear it was deeply felt and poignant. She had stored a couple on her phone. Purely because she had never had anyone write her poetry and it was sort of a memento, also because the originals had weathered over the years to the point of total deterioration. She fumbled on her phone to find them, whilst she waited for Susannah to return from the bar. She had to have a drink after that fiasco and Kirstin needed another.

She remembered she had saved them in a Word document and then e-mailed them to herself. Finally, they were located, and she sat comfortably in the armchair in the small office, rested back her head and silently re-read them, after approximately 35 years.

For you

Once more to feel you next to me
Once more to feel your hair touch mine
The seasons pass; the rain and sun
Can never dull the taste of wine

Can you see in twenty years?
What you and I will be
In love, entwined in each other's arms
Or in love across the sea?

It has no meaning, my lovely
Miles which separate our thoughts
In Tunisia or Istanbul
A love not sold or bought

A love like ours is just a love
And there's no more important words to say
Except that maybe you will have my child
And soon will come the day

The rain may beat upon my soul
Trouble congregates upon my brow
With you I face anything
My love, don't leave me now

The summer sun will once more
See us smiling with our song,
The winter snow may see us cry
But to cry in love cannot be wrong

Time may change our lives, my love
Sorrow and sad songs show our age
But love will keep us one, my love
And these words be upon our grave

SLEEPING TIGER

Words – perhaps two thousand
To express ten million thoughts
Of a love that can't be sold
Of a love that can't be bought

Your eyes show your love and schemes
My eyes show despair and time
Your eyes show your love and its themes
My eyes hope that you are mine

Should my eyes be wrong in what they think?
Should you say No and go away
Should people ask 'why are you alone'
I will answer
'My angel went back to heaven – she could only stay a day'

When all this is said and done, my love
If we ask why we are here
It's because of other people
The ones we hold so dear

To me you are the start and end
To me you are my world
I live for love, I love for you
A dragon and a saint unfurled

One day your dragon will be no more
One day his fire quenched
But not because he lived alone
Not because his hopes were drenched

But because he loved the one and only
Angel who set foot on earth,
Because he had a dream come true
A dream more than he was worth.

Kirstin stopped momentarily, trying to understand the Jekyll and Hyde character of this man. With a sigh, she found the last and final poem, which was untitled. She couldn't recall when either of them was written or what was going on at the time, although the next poem suggests it was when it was all over, but both these indicated quite a different side to Mr Tarrant.

I once knew a kind of love
Which few men ever know,
A kind of love which has no end
A kind of love to grow

But foolishness and ego
Made me toss that love aside,
And now I sit in hotel rooms
Alone with just my pride

Another person came along
And I just wasn't there
You said he didn't mean a thing
He gave you love and care

And slowly you took down the wall
The barrier as well

You gave your body and your soul,
The heaven turned to hell

To hell for me I mean to say
For you, blue turned to gold
You held a lover in your arms
I once had you to hold

And so, my love the time has come
The parting of our ways
There's only one thing left to say
I'll love you all my days

Perhaps from time to time you'll think
About me and my love
For you which never ended
And about our happy home

The home that we just might have built
If things had worked out right
The home I think about right now
In my hotel room, tonight

After a few minutes Kirstin sat up, stretched and tried to shake herself out of this melancholy stupor. The man was truly deluded, she conceded. Susannah returned with the drinks and both women sat silently for a while, savoring normality.

Eventually, Kirstin spoke and passed her mobile to Susannah to show her what she'd been reading. Susannah was speechless and couldn't believe Max had written such caring, emotional prose, particularly for one so full of his own importance. She passed the mobile back to Kirstin and asked her when she was going to delete them. Kirstin responded that she would never do that, as they were for her, they couldn't be duplicated or part of anyone else's life, only hers. Susannah was surprised, as surely what he'd written wasn't worth the paper it was written on. Kirstin disagreed. There was a chink of light in what she'd read, revealing a side of Max Tarrant she'd remembered and once trusted. She'd forgotten it was there, but this was testimony to it. Unfortunately, he turned into a control freak. A self-possessed and arrogant man, oblivious to others' feelings and that's what she'd delete from her mind.

Susannah understood how she felt, Kirstin had been through hell and high water with that man but thankfully she was rid of him. It was just unfortunate that he should re-appear here.

The women finished off their drinks, whilst giggling how the ageing process isn't always kind. Max Tarrant's physical appearance had certainly had a downward slump, poor man. With that cheerful thought, they left the small office and made their way to the restaurant.

It was now quite late, 9.30 p.m., given the interruption with Max Tarrant. Still they were in the Hotel tonight in the Blue Bay Restaurant, so time didn't matter.

Kirstin hadn't booked a table, assuming there wouldn't be a problem. It was Wednesday, a weekday, so probably not as busy. This was indeed the case. There were only around a dozen people in the restaurant, so they could choose exactly where they wanted to sit. They decided on a table in the corner, away from others but still with spectacular views across the bay.

They ordered some wine and water, whilst they perused the menu. Once they had decided, they called over the waiter to order. They'd kept it simple, both choosing to have Mozzarella and Tomato as a starter, followed by a fillet steak with salad.

Susannah took a large swig of wine and promptly opened her clutch bag, whisking out her mobile. Kirstin wondered for a minute what she was doing. Was she going to make a call or send a text to someone? Instead, she pressed a few buttons and passed Kirstin her phone. 'Read that,' she inferred with a flick of a hand. Kirstin took the phone but was a bit perplexed by Susannah's tone of voice and strange request. This seemed to have come out of the blue. Susannah had been fine all evening, well, apart from having heart failure seeing Max Tarrant but other than that, she was in good spirits.

Kirstin cast her eyes down to read what was on the small screen in front of her. Her eyes opened wider as she read on, until they reached the end of the message and refocused on Susannah.

'Guess?' Susannah prompted, before Kirstin could speak. Kirstin had already noticed the initials at the top of the text message and knew immediately this smelt of trouble.

Chapter 22

Greg was about to send a text message to Susannah, when his phone rang. It was an unknown number, but he decided to answer it anyway. It was the police regarding Rob's possessions. Greg wondered why they were mentioning these to him as surely they would be the property of his family. The police officer informed Greg that Rob had no living relatives, which was odd as Rob had said his parents lived in London. The officer continued to enlighten him by stating his parents were both killed in a serious motorway accident six years ago. 'He has no other family. We have been advised by Rob's solicitors Messr's Armitage and Willow to contact you, as you have been named as the main beneficiary, along with your wife.'

Greg was unable to respond. What was going on?

Was this a joke? Beneficiary? What were they talking about? The officer tried to get a response from Greg by repeatedly asking if he was there and could he hear him. Shocked to the core, Greg answered by asking for the details of Rob's solicitors. 'They will be contacting you, sir, but I will give a contact name and their phone number.' Unable to focus, Greg had to have the details repeated three times before they were correct. The officer asked if it was convenient for him to call into the Earls Court Police Station, as soon as possible to collect Rob's items. It was easy to find, located on Earl's Court Road. Greg acknowledged the information and confirmed he would call later in the afternoon. He would leave work slightly earlier than usual and do a detour.

He stared down at the contact name and phone number of the solicitors and although there were several crossings out, it could be deciphered what he'd finally written; Olivia Tweddle, followed by the telephone number. Greg thought he'd better check this out, as it all seemed like a dream, a bad one at that. This couldn't be true surely. Rob would never have made him and Susannah beneficiaries to his estate and certainly not without telling them.

Puzzled by it all, Greg picked up his mobile, now nearly fully recovered from being dead as a dodo and dialed the number he was given.

A receptionist answered and Greg immediately

asked to speak with an Olivia Tweddle. He was requested his name and who or what it was about. Greg gave the information required and waited. After a few moments, a woman's voice at the other end of the phone said she was putting him through.

Ms Tweddle was softly spoken and confirmed she was Rob's solicitor. She had been trying to contact Gregg for a while, but she thought his phone was switched off. This was obviously when it had no power. She asked if he could make an appointment, preferably with his wife. Greg quickly informed her Susannah was his partner, not wife and that she was currently in Monaco. Ms Tweddle indicated this was not a problem at this stage, but she would need to be present nearer the time of finalising transactions. They arranged a meeting for Friday at 8.00 a.m. Greg could call in before work. This was to be a brief meeting initially.

Greg mentioned the call from the police regarding Rob's possessions and that he'd been asked to collect them. He wasn't sure if he should. Ms Tweddle confirmed this was fine and he needed to do this as soon as possible. With that confirmed, the call ended.

It was late afternoon and Greg hadn't achieved anything regarding his work. He made himself a cup of tea and grabbed a biscuit from a tin in the office kitchen. He needed to reply to Susannah's text.

He thought long and hard about what to say, or what not to say would be more like it. He decided not to rock the boat and keep it simple. He would follow by her example. He would not mention anything other than the unpleasant events which had taken place in Monaco and that he was pleased they were both fine. Simplicity was the answer. She was too far away to contemplate trying to explain anything else at this stage and it would be totally unfair to burden her with the current complications. So, he settled to text Susannah a message, whilst sipping his tea, taking a bite of biscuit and hoping he could eventually make it up to her for all this mess.

Dear Susannah,

I could not believe the news when I heard it and was so delighted to hear from you. I am so pleased you are both fine, although what is happening out there must be quite worrying. You seem to be thinking positively and being resilient. The best way to handle it, I think. You will soon be home, just a couple more days. I've missed you so much, we need to catch up on news. We could go up to London for an evening out and stay somewhere overnight for a change. What do you think?

Take very good care of yourselves. See you very soon.

All my love,

Greg xx

Greg re-read the text and thought he sounded a bit over-zealous but he didn't care, he had missed her and yes, they will need to catch up on news. Although, that could be the tricky part. Anyway, he just wanted to make her feel good. He hoped it would work and keep things on an even keel for the time being. With that, he sent the message and prayed.

Within the next hour or two he would leave to go to Earl's Court Police Station. He wasn't looking forward to it or what he was about to receive. This played on his mind more than anything and was not a job for the faint-hearted.

He would then make his way home and probably eat out somewhere, as he didn't think he could face returning home. He had a mass of clearing up, washing and general sorting to complete. It was not going to be the best job in the world. Throwing Rob's toiletries away, washing the bedding, didn't bear thinking about, particularly as Rob was dead. No longer returning to Cleveland Road ever again. This was so hard to believe, and Greg was struggling with it massively. It wasn't sinking in and he wondered if it ever would.

He started thinking about all the people who knew Rob, particularly through sporting activities. He needed to do something, so friends and distant family, cousins, aunts, uncles could be informed. He could put an advertisement in the Telegraph maybe. People did that sort of thing quite often, so perhaps he would do this in the next couple of days. It was the best he could do for now. Once he could access more information about Rob, through whatever means became available to him, he would deal with this more specifically.

Greg's whole thought process was entirely taken up with Rob and he felt a need to talk out loud to someone. Susannah would be his first choice but that would be a difficult situation altogether and one that couldn't happen for a few more days either. Perhaps he ought to go up to the golf club, where he was sure to meet up with people who knew Rob, many of whom would be unaware of what had happened. This may help him too, to reconcile what had happened and make it reality.

Time passed quickly and he needed to make his way to Earl's Court Police Station. He knew roughly where it was on Earl's Court Road, so once he was there it would be easy to locate. On the spur of the moment, he decided to take a cab, as he felt reluctant to use the tube. Images of Rob standing on the platform flashed before his eyes and he couldn't face it.

He picked up a cab easily outside Northcliffe House and within 15 minutes he was dropped off at the Police Station. He tentatively went inside and conveyed his reason for calling. Within a few minutes, a tray with items in it appeared on the counter. Greg recognised Rob's rucksack immediately, which had been emptied of his laptop and other personal possessions. Rob's watch and signet ring with the initials RJH (Robert James Harrison) clearly engraved, sat unloved in the bottom of the tray. This was surreal. Greg had never experienced anything like it in his life before and just wanted to walk away. Eventually, the officer produced a list of the items and asked Greg to sign for them. That was it, Rob's daily possessions given away, without sacrifice or feeling. Receiving them was a different matter.

Greg placed everything in a carrier bag that he'd brought with him and left the police station. He made his way back to Barnes, choosing a cab and an overland train. He would drop off home and depending on how he felt would either grab something to eat in or go up to the golf club.

He wouldn't look at any of Rob's possessions until later and only if he could face doing so. He wasn't sure what to do with them anyway but maybe some relations might come to light, once Greg could delve into Rob's background. Not a thought he was relishing.

He arrived at Cleveland Road around 7 p.m. and was hesitant to enter knowing he had to make some sort of a start on things. A systematic approach was called for he decided. He would start by stripping the bed, put the bedding straight into the washing machine and re-make it with clean linen. Then he would take a black sack and put all Rob's toiletries from the bathroom in it and put it outside in the wheelie bin. There were a few clothes too, so they would also go in the black sack. He was certain a charity shop would be grateful of them, but he couldn't handle this.

Once he started, it wasn't as bad as he'd thought. He kept focused and went from one job to another until it was sorted. He would dry the bedding and drop it into to the dry cleaners for pressing in the morning. They opened very early, so this was convenient and would save another job.

As it was approaching 8 p.m., he thought he'd order a takeaway and have it delivered, so he could sit and look through Rob's possessions. He cleared the kitchen of cups, plates, glasses and put them in the dishwasher. It could all go on after his meal tonight. He glanced around to check if things were back to normal, satisfied, he reached for his mobile and ordered a take away. He put plates in the oven to warm through, poured himself a large glass of wine and retreated into the living room.

He pulled over the carrier bag, which he'd lent against a chair as he walked through. He settled to taking everything out and placing it on the oak coffee table. Rob's MacBook Pro laptop, his mobile, a desk diary, two chargers, reading glasses, a paperback book by Stephen King strangely and aptly entitled 'Finders Keepers', his watch and signet ring. Greg sat back and viewed them with serenity. He wondered what to do.

He finally decided to discuss this with the solicitor on Friday. He assumed at some point he would have to visit Rob's house, which was located over the other side of the village green about fifteen minutes away. Maybe there he would find some clues to his past and other members of his family.

For now, he would pack it all away in the carrier and put it out of sight until he was ready to deal with it properly.

There was a knock at the door. It was his takeaway, fittingly timed. He placed the packed carrier in the under-stairs cupboard and closed the door. He greeted the takeaway man cheerfully, paid and retired to the kitchen. Placing his meal in the oven, he poured another large glass of wine and sunk into an armchair.

With a nearby handset, he turned on some soothing and relaxing, easy-listening music and let his thoughts drift. He still couldn't come to terms with his predicament, it was evident it would take time. Until the next part of the jigsaw manifested itself, what was to happen next was anyone's guess.

Greg's jacket lay over the chair next to him, where he had draped it on returning home. He could see something jutting out of the inside pocket. He pondered as to what it was for a minute, then instantly realised it was the letter from Rob. He hadn't handed it to the police, as was his intention but he now felt this wasn't necessary. This was a personal letter to him and although it indicated Rob took his own life, which the police already knew from witnesses, it was Rob's farewell to him, expressing his feelings and love. Greg cherished this and felt it of no interest to the police. Rightly or wrongly, he would put it safely away.

Chapter 23

'I don't have to guess,' remarked Kirstin. What surprised Kirstin more was the calm and collective way Susannah was behaving. This was not typical. Kirstin studied Susannah's beautiful, deep dark brown eyes and noticed a significant depth and determination. Gone was the sheepishness, nervy disposition, very tolerant stance, so frequently displayed, and there sat a very astute, confident woman. Her eyes radiated acceptance of a situation she could deal with.

Kirstin enquired when Susannah had received the text and if she had responded. Susannah proceeded to explain that she had responded but not to the missent text. She had decided to ignore it, as though she hadn't received it and see what sort of acknowledgement she got, if any. Kirstin's eyes widened in disbelief. She had never heard Susannah be so dispassionate about something so close to her heart. It was uncanny. Finally, she was playing Greg at his own game. She was exhibiting a shrewdness beyond credence. Kirstin was proud of her.

Susannah took back her mobile and flipped it shut with the contempt the text deserved. She would know the facts in due course, within a couple of days in fact. Frankly, that would be the sorting of the wheat from the chaff, so to speak. To separate what would be useful or valuable, from what was worthless, was what it amounted to. This rather hostile stance came over Susannah like a pervasive cloud enveloping her, resisting movement or any sway of emotion. She was not going to be intimidated, deceived or broken by anything other than the plain truth or the facts of the matter. It would all have to wait, she was going to enjoy the remaining days of the holiday and whatever the circumstances, they would still be the same when she returned. Her mind was made up and Kirstin was, without doubt, impressed and supportive of her decision. She couldn't quite imagine what had triggered such a response from Susannah over this, but she was pleased. At last her close friend and ally was standing up for herself in the face of adversity.

They ordered some much-needed coffee and a couple of Glenmorangie whiskies. They deserved them, after the ordeals of the day. This final revelation regarding Greg had rather put the icing on the cake, depositing a final end to the evening. It had certainly proved an illuminating day, one way or another. Seeing Max Tarrant was like a rave from the grave but was more grave than rave, as it turned out.

It all amounted to a very long day in fact. What was to be a delightful visit to the Cathedral, turned into a disastrous, frightening and scary experience, where they were not sure at one point if they would be alive to tell the tale. Bombs exploding, men in balaclavas brandishing machine guns, was not for the faint-hearted.

They requested some more coffee, as it was providing a rather pleasant form of recovery from shock and general weariness. They would never sleep with all this caffeine, but it somehow relaxed them in preparation for sleep. Probably when they did eventually get to bed, it would be more like passing out, as they were so tired. The wonderful complimentary massage, offered by the Hotel earlier, had also had a soporific effect on them, so they doubted if more sleep-inducing tactics would be required.

They glanced around the restaurant and realised they were the only ones left. Kirstin checked her watch and was surprised it was now the witching hour; midnight. So, whilst they looked around for witches, demons, ghosts and gremlins to appear, they requested the bill. This arrived with speed, as though staff were waiting to clear the final table and prepare for the morning. Who would blame them? For them it had been an elongated evening, having so few to cater for. This is always the case, the less busy, the longer the duration. Unfortunately, for Susannah and Kirstin this had seemed like two days piled into one.

They left the restaurant and made their way in the direction of the reception area, where they would go their separate ways to their rooms and finally relax and sleep off the tensions of the day.

On reaching the reception area, there was a sudden blast of bodies entering the Hotel. They were a mix of uniformed and plain-clothed officers. Kirstin and Susannah could plainly see most were armed, others probably were too but their weapons were concealed in their clothing. The reception staff were spoken to and indicated they understood.

What was going on? The troop of men and the odd woman officers flew past both women in an aggressive and determined fashion, heading for the stairs. Some veered off to use the lift, indicating a two-pronged attack. Kirstin knew what was coming, she had already briefed herself on what was going to happen, and she was right.

It was all to do with the men in the room near Susannah and it also involved the woman from the

Casino, somehow. Whatever it was, it was about to turn a whole lot worse. Kirstin thought it best for Susannah to come to her room, out of the way of where she thought they were intending to aim for. She quickly grabbed Susannah's arm and yanked her off in the direction of her room.

Without warning, several men came hurtling down the stairs at full pelt, shouting, pushing and shoving each other to get out of the way. Kirstin looked around in horror and immediately recognised them as the men in the Hotel, plus others she couldn't identify. They were heading for the main entrance, exactly where Kirstin and Susannah were stood. The reception staff shouted at them to get out of the way and beckoned them to come behind the reception counter quickly. Kirstin was doing no such thing and whilst still clinging onto Susannah, the pair placed themselves strategically in front of the doors they were heading towards. The reception staff peered above the counter to see what they were doing and kept shouting for them to move. It was too late. The men started to use their firearms. The glass doors and windows were shattered. Kirstin pulled Susannah down with her to the ground. They were unhurt. Just as the men were trying desperately to escape, more officers arrived and at the entrance, the men were forced back into the Hotel. The other officers emerged from upstairs and it became a game of cat and mouse. Guests peeped around corners and bannisters, all over the place to see what on Earth was going on. It was turning into a blood bath and Kirstin and Susannah were trembling with fear. They had sloped behind a large protruding pillar, taking refuge. Suddenly, all the lights went out, the whole place was in total darkness, pitch black. Screaming and pandemonium could be heard all over the Hotel. What now?

Torches could be seen but this was not a good thing. It was providing light and guidance to this gang of men, who were diligently trying to defy the odds against the police. From nowhere, a body stumbled over Kirstin and Susannah, propelling Susannah away from the security of the pillar. Kirstin had no idea if this person was police, enemy or guest. Kirstin asked who they were, ridiculous but essential she thought, but they were clearly more interested in getting out of the place, so pushed her out of the way and headed towards what she assumed was the entrance. It was so black. It was not possible to see what was happening and by this time she was beginning to lose her sense of direction. She didn't know which way to head, or manoeuvre herself. She tried to call out to Susannah but there was so much noise, people shouting in foreign languages, it was impossible.

She put her hand out to try and feel her way around. She crawled on her hands and knees in what she thought was the right direction, although this was not possible to determine now. She heard a scream, so piercing it went through her, she wanted to put her hands to her ears. *Who was that?* she wondered, distressed. She continued to crawl along the floor. Her hand felt an object, it didn't take much of an imagination to conclude it was a handgun. Kirstin placed it in her grip, just in case. She had never held a gun before but there was a first time for everything. With that, she continued feeling her way along the floor. She stopped, as she could see faintly ahead from an outside light, shafting its way through a small window, several bodies lay strewn across the floor. She sat back and lifted herself up to standing. Trembling, she tried to find something to help her balance. She tripped and fell, she realised she was by the main entrance again. There was glass all over the floor and small shards stuck in her hands as she tried to right herself. A large man bowled into her running towards the door, followed by another man. These were the men escaping. She fumbled for the handgun she had acquired and tried to aim it at the last moving target crossing through the doors. She fired the gun, which took all her strength and energy. She could see the uniforms of officers in pursuit of the men and hoped she'd assisted. She lay on the floor exhausted and shocked she had fired the gun. Many people were now rushing out of the smashed doorway and she could hear several sirens in the distance. She would be safe shortly. Susannah, she hoped, was safe too. She couldn't see or hear her voice. The shouting had subsided and there was a quiet calmness substituting the chaos. She called Susannah but there was no response. Lights started to come back on, which made her feel better, although it just highlighted the terrible carnage that lay before her. She knew what had happened and what still was happening in fact, as police were handcuffing and removing people, as well as tending to the injured. It crossed her mind to have alerted this to the authorities earlier, but they wouldn't have taken her seriously. She was only guessing and clutching at straws, she had no real evidence. She had done her best raising it with Max Tarrant. At least he took it seriously. This tonight was probably because he had uncovered something and was following a lead she'd given him. The men in this Hotel were part of something sinister and were most certainly planning operations that would rock this area of Monaco, for whatever reason. It was revenge for something, but killing and maiming innocent people in their wake was not acceptable, blatantly barbaric.

More police and paramedics arrived, immediately assisting and tending to people in need. It was such a horrific site and difficult to identify who were guests and who were gangsters, although the police had around a dozen men in handcuffs, some on the floor injured and others lined up against a wall. Now reenforcements had arrived, these and the walking wounded were marched off.

Kirstin suddenly caught sight of Susannah's dress over the far side of the reception area. She clambered there as quickly as she could, staggering around bodies, shards of glass, broken furniture, all manner of things that had been uprooted from their usual position and dispersed somewhere else. As she got closer, she could see a paramedic tending to Susannah's chest and right arm. The front of her dress was soaked in blood. Susannah had been stabbed in the chest and the top of her right arm. Kirstin dropped to her knees when she reached her and tried to put a comforting arm around her, but Susannah was in too much pain to respond and the paramedic indicated she was going straight to hospital. A stretcher arrived and she was promptly rushed to the waiting ambulance. Kirstin was shaken rigid. She managed to ask which hospital and then she was gone. Susannah was ashen and appeared weak. She was obviously in a very bad state. Kirstin stood for a while propping her hand against a wall. She was unable to move. Shock had set in and she needed to sit down. She felt she was going to faint. Her knees buckled, she slid down the wall and was out.

Sometime later, Kirstin found herself still in the reception area but this time she was sat on a large soft squashy chair. Someone was offering her a nice cup of strong tea and telling her she would soon be feeling fine. She realised she had fainted and wasn't remotely surprised. At that moment, Gladys and Jack appeared in front of her, enquiring if she was all right. She confirmed she was but asked what had happened to them, as both were sporting bandages to their arms and legs. They were apparently caught up in flying glass, as they were trying to evacuate the building. They were superficial wounds, nothing too serious but it had shaken them too. They chatted for a while discussing what had happened and conveying how many guests had been hurt, some seriously injured, in what turned out to be a blood bath in the end.

They were extremely upset to hear about Susannah. They asked Kirstin to give her their love and a big hug, if she was up to it. Kirstin confirmed she would, and relayed Susannah was at The Princess Grace Hospital. As they turned to walk away, Jack spun around, saying he was sorry to hear about Max Tarrant, too. They were gone. What did he mean? He assumed Kirstin knew. She felt herself tighten.

Chapter 24

The situation was now urgent. It was early morning and the Hotel was teeming with people, police, forensics, journalists, photographers and staff trying to clear up and deal with the many needs of guests. It was pandemonium. Kirstin felt much better having had some strong tea and time to come around, but she was extremely concerned about the welfare of Susannah. She would quickly wash, change and call a taxi to take her to the Princess Grace Hospital. It was imperative she knew how Susannah was, as the news of this attack would be all over the world and she needed to inform Greg immediately. Also, Phil would be anxious too, so this needed to be done, as soon as possible.

On her return to reception, things had calmed down a little and there were areas cordoned off and glass windows being repaired. A general feeling of order seemed to have returned. Kirstin requested a taxi to the hospital. The receptionist conveyed there was one waiting at the front door, available immediately. Kirstin hurried outside and climbed into the taxi, giving her destination. She decided to phone Phil from the taxi, before he went to work. She glanced at her watch; it was 7 a.m. *Ideal*, she thought, *he'll be out of the shower, dressed and making himself some breakfast.*

The phone rang out and she wanted him to pick up immediately, but it rang on and on. Finally, he picked up. He was out of breath, as he'd left his phone upstairs by mistake and he was in the kitchen, as she'd predicted, making breakfast. He was instantly concerned, as Kirstin wouldn't usually phone, she would use e-mail or text. His response was one of panic and confusion, as it was only 7 a.m. too, what was she thinking?

Kirstin drew in breath before she blurted out there had been a very serious attack at the Hotel and Susannah had been taken to the hospital with stab wounds to her chest and arm. She explained she was in a taxi on her way to the Princess Grace Hospital. Susannah had been there only a little while, so probably she wouldn't be told much when she got there but Kirstin stressed to Phil it looked serious, especially the chest wound. For a few minutes, Phil just listened and let Kirstin have full flow of what she wanted to say. As she was talking, he went over to the TV, which he hadn't yet turned on. The screen was buzzing with shots of the Monte Carlo Bay Hotel, police, journalists and guests being interviewed. He was pleased he hadn't turned it on earlier. He would have been distraught.

Phil sat down at the kitchen table, whilst he listened to further details from Kirstin about how it had started. His mind was whizzing and, apart from trying to keep calm for Kirstin's sake, he was genuinely bothered about her well-being. She was now on her own too. At her next break for air, Phil intervened and without giving it a moment's thought, conveyed he'd be on the next available flight to be with her.

Kirstin gave a big sigh of relief and promptly burst into tears. She quickly regained her composure, as she had arrived at the Hospital. She told Phil she would be in touch later and would also phone Greg, once she was aware of the latest news about Susannah. Phil was bothered Greg would see or hear the news shortly, so offered to phone him to make him aware and that Kirstin would phone, as soon as possible with news.

Kirstin was grateful for that and said her farewells for the time being. She paid the taxi driver and entered the huge regal and modern-looking hospital. This was the scary bit, she thought. She approached the main reception with strength and determination.

She needed to be strong for Susannah and not cave in or get upset.

She explained the situation to the member of staff and was politely requested to take a seat, whilst she checked for information. Kirstin eagerly listened to as much conversation as she could hear and sat with anticipation as to what was coming next. The receptionist beckoned her over and informed her Susannah was in the operating theatre and would be there some time. She said she was welcome to stay and wait and could possibly move upstairs to another waiting room, near to Susannah's room. Kirstin accepted this and thought she might be able to glean some further information from nursing staff up there. Although, already this was not a positive sign and truthfully Kirstin feared the worst. This was much more serious than anyone was letting on.

Before she made her way upstairs, she quickly sent a text to Phil to say Susannah was not in a good place and was in the operating theatre. Strongly emphasising for Greg to come over to Monaco immediately.

Phil was about to phone Greg when he received the text from Kirstin. He was horrified when he read the information. He phoned Greg's number; it rang out. Phil thought he wasn't going to answer but suddenly he picked up. Phil spent the next few minutes putting Greg in the picture and told him to turn on the TV. Greg hadn't followed his usual routine of turning on the TV this morning, as was still making sure everything was clear of Rob's belongings. He had the bedding all packed up to drop off at the cleaners for pressing.

Greg was in a state of shock when Phil had finished explaining what had happened to Susannah and could see by the images on the TV that things were in a dire state in the Hotel. He thanked Phil for letting him know and said he would see him in Monaco as soon as he could arrange a flight. Greg put down his mobile and held his head in his hands. He was mortified. What if anything happened to Susannah? He couldn't contemplate the thought. He must contact the children, James and Abbie. Although both adults in their thirties, this would be devastating for them to comprehend. It was their mother. It was imperative he do it immediately.

For the next half hour, Greg was comforting James and Abbie as best he could. He explained he was getting himself on a flight as soon as possible and for them not to worry, as he would keep them posted of all information once he arrived. He then contacted work and explained the circumstances. He would keep them informed of any news.

Greg phoned a local travel agent, Sky Travel, and outlined the predicament. They asked to call him back in a few minutes, with some flight times. Greg meanwhile located his passport and went to grab a small case from the top of the cupboard in the bedroom. Everything up there was back to normal. Greg was pleased he had focused on the clearing up job and not left it for longer. It was a godsend in the circumstances.

It took him around ten minutes to pack a few basic items and gather some toiletries together. Anything he found that he'd forgotten, he would buy over there. Speed was of the essence and he needed to be at the bedside of Susannah.

The travel company were good to their word and contacted him in around fifteen minutes. They had flight times available, there were a few choices. Greg wanted the first available flight he could manage, which turned out to be 1 p.m. He would call at the travel agents to collect/pay for his ticket etc. and drop off the bedding at the cleaners for pressing on route.

The flight was from Gatwick, so he would make his way there afterwards. He would have plenty of time. He was beginning to calm down now he had secured a flight. He was anxious to start the journey and to be at Susannah's side, when she most needed him. The issues of the last few days had taken a back seat. He would have to sort whatever needed to be sorted at another time. His focus was Susannah, and nothing was going to change that.

It was twelve forty and Greg was boarding the

plane to Nice. He would transfer to Monaco by taxi. He was hoping, if everything went to schedule, he would arrive at the hospital between five and six o'clock. Meanwhile, he would keep in touch with Kirstin once he'd landed. Greg sat back in his seat, trying desperately to relax. He was pleased when the drinks trolley came around and he could have a large whisky and ice.

Meanwhile, Phil was trying to arrange a flight to Nice from Leeds Bradford airport through a travel agent in Harrogate. He also needed to contact the boys and say what was happening. He was waiting for the travel agents to call back. They were certain there was a flight early afternoon available and were just checking the details. His mobile rang and he assumed it was them returning his call, but it was Tom and George. They had been watching the news and were extremely concerned for Kirstin, as Tom knew she and Susannah were staying there. Phil explained the details and whilst Kirstin was still in shock, Susannah had been seriously injured. Phil tried not to over dramatise, as it wasn't necessary, and they had enough on their plates with organising their mother's funeral. Phil agreed to keep in touch but said he would be away for as long as it took. Fortunately, the funeral was another week away. Both boys passed on their love to Kirstin and hoped she would be okay.

Phil's mobile went again, and it was the travel

agents this time. All plans had been made for a flight at 2 p.m. He had plenty of time to gather what he needed, so he would stroll around to Tower Street, to Number One Travel shortly, to collect his ticket and general information.

He would also pop in to work and have a chat with colleagues regarding what had happened and his requested absence for a few days, until things could be sorted out. He was beginning to feel it was one thing after another. First, Tom with his accident and injuries, followed by Diane and now Kirstin and Susannah. Kirstin of course was still oblivious about Diane and Phil certainly had no intention of enlightening her anytime soon.

Phil arrived at the airport in plenty of time and sat and read his paper until his flight appeared on the monitor. He had texted Kirstin to confirm Greg was on his way and he would keep in touch with her and she knew Phil would be arriving at some time after Greg, so she was comforted by that at least. This was no time to be sat in a foreign country on your own, in a hospital, without information or confirmation that Susannah would pull through.

Kirstin approached the reception area upstairs and informed the person stationed there who she was and who she was waiting for information about. The nurse took details and confirmed Susannah was still in theatre. She pointed to a coffee lounge further down the corridor and promised she would call her when there was any news concerning Ms Kingsley.

Kirstin sighed and turned around to head down the corridor. It was going to be a long wait, perhaps she would collect herself a magazine or paper to read from the kiosk. She would get herself a coffee first though, as she was parched.

As she was working out how to use the coffee machine, a voice came from behind her, asking if she wanted to join them. It was Olivia. She pointed over to where her husband, Joe, was sitting, together with Felicity and Ed. Several other guests from the Hotel were also milling about, as several people had suffered minor injuries, some major.

Kirstin was delighted to see people she knew and grabbed her coffee after struggling with the technology of the machine and set to join them. Fortunately, the four of them had only minor cuts, bruises and sprains but they were immediately concerned for poor Susannah, whom they had heard was seriously injured. Kirstin confirmed there was no further news but that both her husband and Susannah's partner, were on their way over now.

Olivia expressed her sadness for the man who had helped them in the crisis in the Casino last week. 'He didn't deserve being shot. He was so kind and considerate. He found a place for us to take refuge away from the trouble. He was trying his best to stop those Mediterranean men from escaping last night. He nearly managed it too. Most were caught but he was chasing the ringleader, plus his henchman and someone took him out.'

Kirstin, put her cup down and stared at Olivia. Was she talking about Max? Olivia continued talking but Kirstin could no longer hear her, she could only watch the movement of her mouth. She tried to rise above the black line that was about to blot out her vision. She tried to stop it, but she had no control. She fainted, crashing to the floor and hitting her head on the corner of the table. There was blood everywhere. Nurses were quickly called over to assist. The guests from the Hotel, who were sat with her, were astonished and had no idea what had caused Kirstin to faint.

Within a few moments, staff had brought Kirstin around and were tending to her injury, which they confirmed needed stitches. Gradually, they got her to her feet and were leading her away. She suddenly stopped. She turned, and with agony on her face, asked if he was dead.

Chapter 25

Greg was now well on his way to Nice. His mind of course was still in total confusion. He'd hardly had time to consider the implications of what Rob had done, making him the sole beneficiary of his estate. There was also the problem of getting over Rob. He had cared for him very much and was feeling the true devastation of his death. What was worse was not being able to discuss it with anyone. He needed to talk. In fact, he felt he needed counselling. He could not go through the next few months pretending nothing had happened. He also wanted to be truthful to Susannah. It was only fair. If she felt that there was nothing left of their relationship, then so be it. He could not make her choose otherwise.

What he was sure of was that he wanted to marry Susannah. The relationship with Rob, although one of closeness, was not one of true love, which he had realised the hard way. By putting their relationship on the line, it had brought him to his senses but was this too late? He could only hope when he explained everything to Susannah, she still cared for him.

Greg closed his eyes, manifesting a vision of Susannah. How utterly stupid he had been in the past. Pigheaded, came to mind. What a complete waste. Making this up to her would be his life purpose, if she would have him that was.

His mind drifted back to the solicitor, Ms Tweedle, whom he had arranged to meet on Friday, tomorrow in fact. Obviously, that wasn't going to happen. He would have to call her or send an e-mail. He would want Susannah there too, so the meeting would have to be postponed anyway. There were too many variants, too many bits to join together, to make it all work again. He blamed himself, of course. He had created the whole dreadful mess. He wasn't proud of himself. He didn't want to tell the children but what if Susannah wouldn't accept him back into her life? He couldn't imagine it. He also couldn't imagine his children knowing the reason why either. He would feel beyond reproach. It was his own fault.

Greg continued to torture himself over the goings-on of the last few days, but his focus needed to change and change rapidly. His only focus now should be Susannah's welfare.

*

Phil was also in the air, travelling to Nice but slightly later than Greg. It was a bizarre situation. This all started out as a pre-birthday celebration for Kirstin, which would have been over by Saturday. Who knew when this would end. Phil was keen to establish the facts and to find out exactly what the prognosis was about Susannah's condition and until that was clear, nobody could make any decisions.

He was anxious to be with Kirstin, as he felt she was not disclosing everything and that something was wrong. He felt she was shielding him from something, and he didn't want her to take the burden of whatever it was. He'd known her long enough to be able to tell when there was something major filling her mind, to the point of destroying her sanity. She was resolute and could handle most things, but he felt she was under pressure, withholding information and at the same time dreadfully concerned about Susannah's condition. How could all this happen on a break away, with the intention of it being a pre-celebration?

No doubt Kirstin would put him in the picture once he arrived and they were at liberty to talk frankly about the goings-on at the Monte Carlo Bay Hotel.

His foremost concern was at what point to tell her about Diane. The whole unadulterated version of the story was somewhat alarming, particularly the bedroom scene. If Kirstin was her usual self, she would probably laugh herself silly at the very thought of Diane hiding in their bed but there was also another side to this, which could prove hard to understand and appreciate. Did he encourage her? Did he desire her again? Was it all a set up? Why had Diane chosen to do this? Did she desire him still? It could all be taken out of context and not look good for Phil, at all. He did have Tom though. He knew nothing had been pre-planned or stage-managed by Phil, only by his mother. He didn't know about the bedroom scene, although Phil was concerned that he had heard but he could be wrong.

Why Phil was worrying about it, he wasn't sure, but he was unhappy about not being able to tell Kirstin at the time. She would understand that, he was sure. Just as he would have to understand whatever had been happening in Monaco, unbeknown to him.

He couldn't wait to be with Kirstin again, although it had only been a relatively short time, it had been very eventful for both. The testing of time apart was soon to be rectified and he felt safe in the knowledge that none of the goalposts would have changed. Kirstin would be, as she always was, his wife and steadfast buddy.

Greg had landed and was in a taxi heading towards the Princess Grace Hospital. He was very apprehensive as to what he was going to face. He needed to text Kirstin to see if there had been any further developments. He took out his mobile and tapped out a message to her. It read: -

Hi Kirstin,

I'm in a taxi on my way to you at the hospital. Have there been any further developments concerning Susannah's condition?

Greg x

He sent it immediately and hoped she'd reply quickly, so he would be prepared of what to expect when he arrived.

Kirstin was having eight stitches put in the side of her forehead. She was exceedingly shaken by her fainting episode and even more fraught to gather something serious had happened to Max Tarrant. The nurse was just putting a dressing over the stitches, so they wouldn't catch on anything. Kirstin had a belting headache, which was due to the crack to her head and probably to her worry and concern about Susannah and Max. Was she truly worried and concerned about Max? Yes, she was. You can't marry and live with someone for ten years and not feel some compassion. There was also the support during the early years. The protection, both physically and mentally. Yes, there was all the heartbreak too and that killed it, but it didn't mean she couldn't be sorry he was hurt or even dead. She didn't know yet. Just the thought overwhelmed her, and she could feel tears stinging her eyes. The nurse queried if she was all right. She asked if the stitches were hurting her. Kirstin said she was fine and just needed a coffee and to take a painkiller.

Kirstin asked where her bag was and the nurse duly passed it to her, from a chair in the corner of the room. Kirstin checked her phone and instantly saw Greg's text message. She quickly replied.

Hi Greg,

So pleased you will soon be here. There has been no word from the medical staff as to how Susannah is but considering the length of time, I think it won't be too long before we hear. Unfortunately, I've just had a gash to my forehead sewn up. I fainted! Explain all when you get here. One calamity after another!

Kirstin x

Greg read Kirstin's reply just as the taxi was pulling up outside the hospital. He couldn't believe something else had happened to poor Kirstin and was somewhat dismayed that nothing more had transpired on Susannah's condition.

He was eager to get inside the hospital, so speedily paid the taxi driver, gathered his baggage and entered the building. He headed to the main reception and asked where he would find Susannah Kingsley, who was his partner and was currently in surgery. He was directed upstairs, to the area where Susannah was being treated. Kirstin was looking out for him, before venturing back to the coffee lounge. She saw Greg approaching the small reception area, wheeling his case behind him. She called and waved as she moved slowly along the corridor, still feeling slightly wobbly and weak. Greg rushed to meet her and gave her a big hug. After a few minutes of exchanging pleasantries and current information, particularly about Kirstin's head gash, they both approached a nurse at the desk to ask for an update on Susannah. No sooner had they asked, a surgeon appeared from the operating theatre, asking for waiting family and friends. The nurse directed him to Kirstin and Greg. Both introduced themselves. The surgeon asked them to step into a side room. They followed him with trepidation. Once they were all seated, the surgeon, Mr Gillam, explained that surgery had seemingly gone well, although Susannah had lost a lot of blood. She was not out of danger yet. There were two stab wounds to her chest, one more serious than the other, as it was close to her heart. She also had another stab wound to her right arm that was not serious but had required several stitches. He conveyed Susannah was in intensive care and would need to remain there for some time, until her condition showed signs of improvement. Mr Gillam continued to say they could see her shortly, although she wasn't fully conscious, so best see her one at a time. Both Greg and Kirstin nodded their heads in agreement and were somewhat shocked by the seriousness of the surgery required.

As Susannah was not fully conscious, they decided to go and get a coffee. Greg, for his initial shock of learning the current situation and Kirstin, so she could take a painkiller for her banging headache. They walked down to the coffee lounge. Kirstin could see other guests from the hotel still sat around, and Olivia and Felicity with their husbands, but didn't want to re-join them as she needed some time with Greg. She also wanted clarification from those who knew about Max. She didn't want to involve Greg in that conversation. They looked across as she entered the coffee area, waved and shouted was she all right. They could see she was with someone, so said, 'join us later'. Kirstin said she was fine and would be over in a while. Kirstin observed Greg had turned an ashen colour and suggested he sit down, while she got him a hot chocolate to give his sugar levels a boost. Greg agreed. He wasn't expecting the seriousness of Susannah's injuries. Phil hadn't elaborated deliberately but also; he didn't know the severity of her injuries. In fact, neither did Kirstin, as she never saw her properly before she was whisked off to the hospital. Her dress was soaked with blood, so she had feared the worst but hearing the extent of her injuries was still horrific.

They sat together and chatted until Greg started to feel better. Kirstin took her painkiller and hoped it would soon do the trick. Greg was anxious to see Susannah, so Kirstin suggested he go and sit with her until she fully came around. She would go back and sit with the hotel guests and then pop along later. Kirstin was expecting Phil to arrive within the hour, so she would keep tabs on her phone meanwhile.

Greg sauntered back down the corridor to intensive care. Kirstin could see how upset and helpless he seemed. It had been a real shock for him and sitting with her would be the best thing he could do. She would need someone familiar to be there, when she fully awakened.

Kirstin grabbed the rest of her coffee and moved back across to join Olivia and Felicity. Their husbands had both just been called to have their cuts and gashes attended to. They weren't serious but they needed proper medical attention. Olivia and Felicity had superficial injuries, bits of glass stuck in hands and feet, the odd graze and bruising but they had been checked, treated and were fine.

Kirstin plonked herself down between them and both asked about her forehead. She explained she'd had eight stitches and apart from a headache she was fine. Kirstin quickly re-established their previous conversation about Max and asked Olivia what she meant about Max being taken out. Olivia proceeded to explain she had been told by one of the SAS men that Max was in pursuit of the gang's ring leader and his henchman, when from nowhere a bullet from behind hit him in the head. They were all running out of the main entrance of the Hotel. Olivia had asked about his condition whilst at the hospital and it was confirmed to her, he was in an induced coma.

Kirstin could only hear the words, 'all were running out of the main entrance of the Hotel, when a bullet came from nowhere'.

She had shot a bullet from nowhere, thinking it was the gangsters escaping.

Had she shot Max?

Chapter 26

Whilst Kirstin was sat contemplating whether she had shot Max, her mobile gave a ping. Casting her eyes momentarily to check it, she saw it was Phil. *At last, he's here*, she thought closing her eyes with relief. Now she would be fine. Kirstin excused herself from the company of Olivia and Felicity and went to the main reception area to meet Phil. She could see him stood just inside the doorway, still staring at his phone.

As she neared, he looked up and caught sight of her approaching. His whole demeanour altered. He was smiling, uplifted and enthusiastic. He greeted her with a big hug and a kiss. He put his arm around her shoulder, whilst examining the large gash to her forehead. They walked towards the downstairs coffee area, as Kirstin didn't want to return to the one upstairs for the moment. She wanted some undisturbed time with Phil on her own.

They grabbed some coffee and retreated to an area where there was no one nearby. Phil asked how she was feeling, as she looked pale and drawn, although he didn't say this exactly. She admitted it had all been a terrible shock, she was beside herself with worry about Susannah and the additional gash to her head hadn't helped. Her headache hadn't gone, and she was still in turmoil over the thought she had shot Max. She wasn't mentioning the latter, of course. Phil was totally unaware that Max Tarrant had re-appeared in Kirstin's life and she was going to keep it that way until she was ready.

They sat and chatted about mundane issues. Neither was ready to discuss anything other than the basics, so kept the conversation general about flights and the rooms at the Hotel being doubles, so no alterations necessary to accommodation for either Phil or Greg. Although, Kirstin thought Greg would probably be staying at the hospital overnight, considering Susannah's condition.

Whilst Phil was finishing his coffee, Kirstin thought she had better go and see whether Greg was okay and if Susannah was conscious. She so wanted to see her and if Greg was okay with it, probably he could talk to Phil, whilst Kirstin could see Susannah.

Kirstin hurried back up the stairs to the small reception and asked if she could see Susannah. The nurse looked at her slightly awkwardly and proceeded to say that her partner had been looking for her in the coffee lounge. Kirstin couldn't grasp what she was indicating. Several minutes seemed to pass by without anyone saying anything but Kirstin suddenly heard Greg say, 'Kirstin, there you are.' She flew around and looked at Greg directly in the eyes.

'What's happened?' she murmured.

'They have taken her back down to theatre, as an emergency, internal bleeding.'

Kirstin took hold of Greg and pulled him towards her, squeezing him tightly. Both were in tears and needed to move to a private area for a few minutes. Greg accepted a tissue Kirstin rifled out of her bag and dabbed at his eyes. Kirstin, also with tissue in hand, did the same. They were both wrecked by this development. Greg confirmed Susannah had rallied and seemed quite good. They had just started to talk, when suddenly all hell broke loose, beepers were buzzing, and she appeared to faint. Doctors were there immediately and took her back down to theatre.

Kirstin explained Phil was here and they had been sat downstairs. She suggested he come down with her and she would tell the reception where they were if needed, otherwise they would check back with them shortly. Greg agreed and followed Kirstin like a forlorn lamb down the stairs.

Phil stood up immediately, he saw Greg but could see there was a problem. Both men embraced each other and sat down. Kirstin was left to explain what had happened. Greg had gone to pieces and couldn't speak.

Somebody had to take the bull by the horns and do something. This situation was unbearable. Kirstin suggested Phil take Greg back to the Hotel in a cab, they could both have access to their rooms, unpack, have a wash/shower and probably a large drink. She would stay at the hospital and monitor what was happening and report back. There was absolutely no point in them all sitting around becoming more upset and depressed. It wasn't helping anyone, least of all poor Susannah. She needed everyone to keep upbeat and refreshed. She wouldn't want to see others upset and looking wrecked.

Both men agreed, fortunately. The wear and tear was getting to them. So far it had been a very long day. Emotional and mental strain was evident all round. Kirstin walked with them to the main door, kissed and hugged them both and waved as they walked to the taxi rank. She reassured them she would be in regular contact with any updates.

Kirstin re-appeared at the small reception upstairs

to ask if there was any news on Susannah. The nurse disappeared into a room along the corridor to find out. She was only a few minutes. She returned saying the surgeon had said she was out of danger and would be brought back up in a while but that she would be unable to see anyone, as she required time to recover. Kirstin inquired what the length of time might be? Possibly several hours, was conveyed to her. Kirstin thanked the nurse and double checked she had all the necessary mobile contact numbers, if needed. That confirmed, Kirstin texted both Phil and Greg the update. She also said she would be returning to the Hotel shortly. They could decide later whether to return to the hospital in a few hours but would phone first.

Kirstin had one more situation to sort out before she left the hospital, and that was to see Max Tarrant. She returned downstairs to the main reception. She had just started to explain who she was in relation to Max Tarrant, when someone tapped on her shoulder. She angrily turned around. She was not happy being caught mid-sentence, in what was becoming a very complicated explanation of who she was and why she wanted to see Max Tarrant. The person staring at her was Ricardo Lucca. What on earth was he doing here?

Ricardo apologised for startling her but he wanted to interrupt, as he'd heard her mention Max and he wanted to explain. Kirstin excused herself from the desk and moved away to talk to Ricardo. What on earth did he want to say to her? She couldn't imagine. She didn't know him and why would he know about Max Tarrant?

Ricardo apologised again. He said she wouldn't have realised at the time, but he was a special agent working with Max at the Casino. He had been working there some time. They were on to the Mediterranean gang, who were suspected terrorists. They were under surveillance and all was going well but they hadn't realised until it was too late that they had an inside informer and confidante. She ruined their cover and an opportunity to arrest them. She was the woman Kirstin had seen pass the slip of paper to a customer that evening, spotted in the pub, drinking with a Mediterranean man and again later in the hotel, drunk.

Well, well, well, she thought. She knew her gut feelings were correct. She had her suspicions about her from the start. So, what happened that night? Apparently, they had a tip off that they were to bomb the Monte Carlo Bay Hotel. Consequently, the sudden influx of armed officers, which started the whole charade of events. What resulted was the current situation they all found themselves in.

Kirstin lent against a nearby wall and sighed. 'What has happened to Max?' she asked unequivocally.

Ricardo moved closer to her and put his hand on her shoulder.

'I knew all about you. Kirstin. Max told me and he also told me to provide you and your friend Susannah with the complimentary voucher for the meal in Le Salon Rose. He bought that for you. It was just a kind gesture, he wanted to give you.'

Kirstin's eyes filled with tears. 'So, what's happened to him Ricardo?' she persisted.

'As he was chasing the ring leader and one of his henchmen out of the Hotel, he was shot in the head.' Kirstin went as cold as ice, as she embraced the thought. She knew he was in an induced coma, which she reiterated to Ricardo. He knew of course and what he wanted to say was they had brought him round. He was conscious and would she like to see him?

Kirstin felt faint. She wondered what else could possibly happen. Had she shot him? Should she come clean and tell Ricardo what happened? It was killing her not telling anyone. She grabbed Ricardo's hand and squeezed it tightly.

'I think it was me,' she said lamely.

'What do you think was you, Kirstin?' asked Ricardo bemused.

Kirstin went on to describe that night and exactly what happened to her and Susannah. Ricardo was stunned that they were right in the middle of it all. He hadn't realised.

'It definitely wasn't you, Kirstin,' continued Ricardo.

'How can you be so sure?' Kirstin blurted out. 'I shot through the entrance as two men ran through the doorway. It must have been me.' Kirstin was now in tears and sobbing quite loudly. Ricardo tried his best to comfort her, but this was the final straw, she was broken. She had killed someone, and it just had to be Max, of all people. Her ex-husband. Her back slid down the wall until she was sat on the floor, no longer caring what she looked like, or who was staring. She didn't care. What had she done? Why had she shot willy-nilly into the darkness? How stupid was that?

Ricardo was kneeling at her side. 'Kirstin. please listen,' he stressed. 'Max was shot with a bullet from a machine-gun, not a hand gun, as you have just described. The hand gun was found and eliminated. We didn't know whose it was, but it wasn't the gun involved with the shooting of Max. We discovered several bullets in walls outside. That's where your bullet went Kirstin. In the wall!'

Kirstin looked up at him, her face awash with bits of black mascara and gold eyeshadow, which she had applied with care that morning to make herself look and feel better.

'In the wall,' she repeated. 'Are you sure?'

'Absolutely,' confirmed Ricardo.

'Now, do you want to see Max?' Ricardo asked with a smile.

Kirstin clambered to her feet but insisted she needed to go to the bathroom to freshen herself up first. She would be five minutes. Ricardo said he'd wait by the stairs, where there was some seating. He was beginning to feel weary and wanted to rest his legs.

Kirstin was not long, as she had promised. She was looking back to normal and was ready to face Max. She felt immense relief to be sure she hadn't shot Max. A weight had been lifted from her shoulders. There were now no guilty feelings.

She met up with Ricardo and they walked upstairs and along to a private room, at the far end of the building. A police officer stood outside. Ricardo spoke to him and Kirstin was free to enter. Ricardo said he'd wait down the corridor for her.

Kirstin tapped gently on the door before entering. A nurse opened it and beckoned her in. 'He's asked for you,' she said politely. *How strange,* she thought, *why would he think of asking for me?* The nurse closed the door. It was silent. It was dimly lit and rather soothing. Max lay in the bed, not moving and with bandages around his head. There were tubes everywhere, machines clicking and twitching, lights twinkling and occasionally flashing. It was a therapeutic sanctuary of calm.

Kirstin sat gingerly close to the bed and put her hand on Max's. He stirred but didn't say anything. She felt awkward, not sure what to say, if anything. A few seconds passed. She stared at his face. The face she had stared at for many years. Her eyes traced the shape and angle of his eyebrows, the aquiline nose and fullness of his mouth. Nothing had altered. The strength and determination in his jaw line, were all the same.

She softly said his name, telling him it was Kirstin. He stirred again but this time with more vigour and purpose. Very slowly, he opened his eyes. She stared into them, this time with love and care, not anger and hostility. He squeezed her hand and mouthed he was sorry. With great effort, he lifted his other hand and blew a long gentle kiss to her. She smiled and squeezed his hand gently, reciprocating the gesture.

He closed his eyes slowly. His hand lost its grip in hers. He was gone.

Chapter 27

Phil and Greg arrived back at the Hotel Monte Carlo Bay and were extremely impressed with its location and majestic appearance. Kirstin had already informed the Hotel of the arrival of both her husband and Susannah's partner, so they were welcomed at reception as they checked in. There were obviously repairs still being made and there was still a police presence but other than that, it was business as usual. Staff provided a mini tour of the downstairs areas and then showed them to their designated rooms.

Both decided to have a shower and meet in the Blue Gin bar at 8 p.m., which was around the time they expected Kirstin to be back. Phil had tried lightening the mood on the way back from the hospital with general chit-chat, but Greg wasn't in a good place and was reluctant to converse at all. He wanted to be back at the hospital, so he was there if needed. Phil understood and agreed but suggested he freshen himself up, have a drink and perhaps something to eat and to go back a bit later when they had some news.

Greg knew he was right, and it would preserve his energy levels as it had been an extremely long day. There was no good in feeling exhausted when he needed to be on top form to support Susannah. Mentally and physically, he felt rock bottom, but it wasn't all to do with Susannah. He still had everything else whirling round in his head and how he was going to cope with it all, which reminded him he needed to send Ms Tweedle an e-mail. He grabbed his mobile and settled in a comfy chair to think what to say. It read: -

Dear Ms Tweedle,

I am so sorry but I'm afraid I'll have to cancel our appointment tomorrow morning. I'm in Monaco, where my partner has been seriously injured. You have probably seen the media coverage, concerning the terrorist attacks there recently.

I cannot say when I will be returning at this stage, so best to leave the situation until I can let you know another date/time.

Sorry for any inconvenience caused. I will be in touch.

Best wishes,

Greg Morton

Greg pressed send and was pleased he had remembered to let her know. It wouldn't have been fair not to turn up without some form of message being sent as to the reason why. That done, he unpacked the few items he'd brought and had a long warm shower. He did feel much better afterwards. He changed and decided to go and sit in the Blue Gin bar and wait for Phil. It was about 7.45 p.m., so he would have a few minutes alone to ponder but wanted to be around other people, rather than on his own. Being in his own company wasn't helping. He soon became depressed, despondent and full of despair about the future and where it was all going to end.

He arrived in the bar and ordered a large gin and tonic with loads of ice. He sat by a small table by the terrace, overlooking the sea. How beautiful it was. He understood why Susannah was having such a good time here, it was truly bliss. He sat in silence, sipping his drink and praying that Susannah would pull through. They could be happy again, he felt sure but there was a long way to go and many bridges to build, before harmony would resume.

At that moment, his mobile pinged. It was a message from Kirstin. It read: -

Hi Greg/Phil,

I have just been called back to Susannah's ward, where she has returned from theatre. Everything is fine, all has gone to plan. She's going to be all right! The surgeon is suggesting no visitor's until tomorrow, to give her chance to recover slowly. This is great news. Thank heavens. I will see you both soon. Meet you in the Blue Gin bar.

Love Kirstin xx

Greg re-read the text a couple of times, to make sure he'd taken it in. 'Thank heaven indeed,' he mouthed under his breath. He was ecstatic with joy; salty tears plopped into his drink. He could feel the release of tension. It was an incredible weight off his shoulders. He just couldn't manage without Susannah and he was going to make sure she knew that very soon.

*

The beepers sounded and Kirstin was interrupted, whilst resting her head on hers and Max's hand. She was sobbing and it was probably best she did not spend any more time in that situation. Ricardo came to her aid once she appeared at the doorway. He put his arm around her shoulders and walked her slowly to some nearby seating. She fumbled for tissues from her bag and tried desperately to stop the tears. This was just awful. How could everything end like this? What a waste. What a mess of people's lives. All manner of thoughts circulated her brain and they were all questions of why.

She never in her wildest dreams thought she'd ever

see Max Tarrant again, yet here she was, years down the line witnessing his death. An impossible realisation she wouldn't bestow on anyone. This was out of the blue, unexpected and brutally harsh to come to terms with. Although they were no longer married, nor had seen each other for years, it was like losing a best friend, so close the relationship had been at one time.

Ricardo had gone for some water. She waited, still and pre-occupied with her own thoughts. She calmed and was feeling better. Ricardo dutifully returned with the water and sat back down beside her. He took her hand and asked if she was okay. He knew Max didn't have long and Max had asked for Kirstin several times, so he was pleased she was there for him at the end.

As she was sat recovering, a nurse came over to her, explaining Susannah had returned from theatre and Mr Gillam would like to speak with her. Kirstin was fearing the worst, as could be seen by the ultimate pain crossing her face. The nurse instantly put her hand on her shoulder as comfort and conveyed Susannah was fine. Kirstin took a deep breath and stood up ready to follow the nurse back to the ward. She and Ricardo fiercely hugged each other. She thanked him for his kindness, and they parted.

Walking back to the ward seemed the longest walk ever. She was extremely weary, not because she was tired, just emotionally and mentally drained. Mr

Gillam was waiting for her at reception and beckoned her into his private consulting room. He closed the door behind her and indicated for her to take a seat. Kirstin duly sat and waited with bated breath, as to what exactly Mr Gillam was going to say.

He gazed over his half-rimmed glasses and cast his extraordinary, enormously pale blue eyes upon her. Somewhat perplexed by this vision and interrogative stance, Kirstin felt very uncomfortable. She clumsily blurted out whether Susannah was out of danger. He sat back and for a few seconds didn't react. Then calmly came the words. 'She's an incredibly lucky lady to have survived.' The words were so powerful. Kirstin could feel goosebumps and a shudder down her spine. This man was saying; 'she wasn't meant to live and fought a gargantuan battle to beat the odds over death. My goodness, praise indeed. Where did she find the strength? She wouldn't give up, that's why.' Susannah often gave the impression of being meek and mild, but she had a hidden inner strength, which when called upon blew everyone away, as they didn't believe she had it in her.

Mr Gillam sat forward and perched his elbows on the edge of the desk, again giving Kirstin a steely glare over his half-rimmed glasses. 'A resilient lady,' he continued. 'She will require around the clock care for a while,' he emphasised emphatically. 'No visitors until tomorrow,' he ordered. He duly stood up, shook

Kirstin's hand and was gone. His door banged shut and Kirstin sat staring at the wall, as if she'd just been sentenced to something.

Of course, she was over the moon at the news and would text Greg and Phil immediately, but she felt as though she was on a giant rollercoaster. One minute up and the next minute down. Her stress levels were certainly up, and she knew it was time for her to go back to the Hotel before she had a breakdown, literally. She quickly sent her text message and walked downstairs to the main entrance, where she could see a line of cabs.

She knew once she was back at the Hotel, she would be fine. She wasn't going to do any explaining about anything tonight, that was for sure. As Greg wouldn't be returning to the hospital tonight, they could all chill and have a lovely meal together. Susannah had turned the corner and she was going to be all right, everyone would be able to relax and recover from what had been a long, unsettling day.

The cab dropped Kirstin off at the Hotel and she made her way to the Blue Gin bar. She could see Phil and Greg sat over by the terrace. A good spot she thought, away from others and with good views out to sea. Slowly but surely, she could feel the tension leaving her body, she relaxed her shoulders and moved across the bar to meet them. A waiter caught sight of her arriving and asked if he could bring a drink over for her.

'A large glass of Pinot Grigio with ice, would be just perfect,' she requested with a smile.

The two men stood up as she approached the table, and both gave her a hug and a kiss. They were pleased to see her and grateful for the message she had sent. They were all so relieved about Susannah. It was a real touch and go situation and one nobody would wish to be in. It had brought so many emotions to a head. Unfortunately, there was still turmoil to sort out. Some were not aware of what was ahead and what they would need to embrace. It was clear there would be tough times and hard-to-imagine situations for some to comprehend, but what was important was truth and honesty. To rectify and build what was broken was no easy feat, but it could be done. With the help and support of family and friends, together with a determined effort, nothing was unsurmountable. All four of their lives has been turned upside down, in different ways. There were solutions and ways forward for all. They just needed to be found.

Epilogue

How different lives were before the celebration trip. Substitute different for normal, or even complacent maybe. What does it take for one set of values to move drastically to another, in such a short space of time? Human error, maybe, once realised. Time to rectify.

Kirstin never got over the hurt, deceit and humiliation of what Max Tarrant did to her, but she finally put it to rest through a process of eliminating her guilt and an awakening of strength. Max ruled by coercive controlling methods, which severed the relationship long ago. There was no way back. His true feelings were only apparent, too late. Phil was her saving grace.

Kirstin and Phil made time over the following days, on their return to the UK, to let their stories unfold, without compromise. It was what it was. Unintentional, on both counts, none of it was planned. They got on with their lives.

Diane's funeral came and went, and her ashes scattered at Burnmouth, organised by Tom and George. Tom moved back to London to be with Lucy, who fully recovered from the miscarriage. Both were positive for the future and intended to get married next year. George moved to London, close to Tom. He had another job with a high-ranking architect's firm, in the city and was ecstatically happy.

Susannah was recovering in the Princess Grace Hospital, Monaco. She received many visitors from the Hotel, which assisted her recovery. She was making steady progress. Greg was with her every day and was planning a holiday at the Hotel, after she was discharged from hospital, to help her recoup. Greg had proposed but not before telling Susannah the whole truth and nothing but the truth. This was the hardest, most emotional conversation he'd ever had, and he was far from proud of his actions. They talked it through over several days and both accepted there were problems on both sides. They were getting married at the end of the year.

Rob left Greg half a million pounds approximately, together with his property. Greg would help their children and grandchildren financially in ways he would never have thought possible. He was extremely grateful for Rob's friendship and generosity.

Susannah's close friend Celia Harrison sent a letter to Susannah in hospital when she heard the dreadful news. She'd met someone else, since moving closer to her family, who was quite the opposite, thankfully, to her husband Ray, who incidentally, was still in prison for his controlling antics. Her divorce was going through. Susannah and Kirstin were both very happy for her.

The Sleeping Tiger awoke and roared in every single one of their lives, causing untold questioning and the facing of realisations they hadn't ever considered. Now, there was no roar. No anger. No fight. It was gone. It was over and better lives have transformed.

ABOUT THE AUTHOR

The author has been teaching for many years and has observed on numerous occasions the power of the written word and how it can capture the imagination and interest of both young people and adults. She says encapsulating people's attention in this way promotes learning, life experiences and the promotion of self-development and self-worth.

Printed in Great Britain
by Amazon